Play
DIRTY
JORDAN'S GAME
JA HUSS

JORDAN'S GAME
BOOK FOUR

ISBN: 978-1-944475-56-7

Edited by RJ Locksley
Cover Design by JA Huss

DEDICATION

For all the players.
Because you can't win if you don't play.

CHAPTER ONE

How Alexander and I got to this moment really isn't the point. It's not. We're here. He's got his hand on my cock, squeezing it, only the fabric of my pants separating us.

His eyelids are heavy, but I know him. They always look like that. He could be watching the last innings of the final game of the World Series and his eyelids would still be heavy.

So the look on his face means nothing.

He could be turned on, or not.

He could be doing this for me.

Or her.

Or himself.

None of this is the point.

The only point is… I need him and he needs me, and either we find a way to get through this or we all lose. He will lose her, I will lose the Club, she will walk away and life will probably implode.

Dramatic, I know. I get it. But it feels honest.

"Should I kiss you?" Alexander asks.

I have so many things to say back to him right now, it's ridiculous. But none of them are the point either, so I just reach up, grab his hair, and pull him in until our lips meet.

He's not gay.

He's a little bit bi, which is why he's here with me. And I'm a lot bi. Which is why I'm here with him.

But this kiss isn't anything spectacular.

It's rather stiff, actually. His lips don't meld with mine. There's no tongue. There's no moaning or anything like that.

Fingers thread through my hair.

Not his.

Hers.

Her nails are long and today they're painted a deep, shiny red. She presses them against my scalp—lightly—as her lips join ours.

Alexander changes immediately. First, a sigh. Then he moves closer to me. His hand gripping my cock tighter. His mouth softer, his breath faster, his eyes closed.

We kiss like that for a long time, it seems. No one is undressed. No one makes a move to undress.

We just kiss.

Which is a little bit nice. I guess. Kinda high-school. Kinda innocent.

But I'm not really out for a little bit nice.

I want to take her over to the couch, lay her back against the cushions, and fuck her like a man in a threesome.

And hell, her husband is welcome. Like I said, I'm a lot bi. So I welcome that part.

He, however… well, let's just say he doesn't feel the same way.

"You used to like this," Augustine says, kissing Alexander's neck now.

He doesn't open his eyes and I'm grateful. Because he kinda fascinates me and those heavy-lidded eyes come with an intense gaze when they're open.

It gives me an opportunity to look at him.

"I only ever did it for you," Alexander replies. "It was always you who liked this."

I could make him change his mind. I could. I'm that good. But I've given up on the dream of a bonded threesome.

Those feelings have long since passed. I live in a reality of my own making. Which might not be a hundred percent real these days, but it's a lot more realistic than Alexander ever getting used to the idea of *me*.

I grab his hand and remove it from my cock.

This is enough to make him open his eyes.

"What are you doing?" Augustine asks.

"Leaving," I say.

And I do.

I go home. Which isn't a home. I live in a seven-million-dollar, ten-thousand-square-foot historical mansion next door to the Denver Botanical Gardens. I bought it last fall in foreclosure with the hope of…

What?

What was I hoping?

I live here now because I'm liquidating. I have hopes and dreams too. I need things. It's all I've got left and I don't want it unless…

There are seven bedrooms, eleven bathrooms, two media rooms, two offices, two kitchens, a game room, a library, and a ballroom.

And I live here alone.

There's nowhere to drop my keys as I come in the front door because the place is empty. A family lived here before their luck changed. And they left everything behind when they sold it. Even photographs. The happy couple on their wedding day. Pictures of their kids, and I can only assume they did that because they have digitals in Dropbox or some shit, because that part is pretty cold.

Pretty.

Fucking.

Cold.

(But who am I to judge?)

They left everything like it was a holiday home and whatever they kept there was just… extra. Like they went shopping and bought two of everything and so all this was just the spare set.

Except it wasn't.

But it's all gone now. I packed up the photographs in a box and gave them to Lawton. Did he ever return them? I have no idea because I never asked. Then I sold all the furniture in an estate sale last month and bought a desk and a couch from IKEA and had it placed in the fifteen-hundred-square-foot office on the main floor.

I'm pretty sure the IKEA delivery people thought I was crazy, but I don't care. And anyway, it might be true.

I live in the office. I don't even bother using the main kitchen because I don't cook and the office has a wet bar—because all gentlemen who own ten-thousand-square-foot-homes have a wet bar in their office—and it even has a dishwasher to wash the cut-crystal glasses I drink bourbon out of every night before bed, so who cares about the industrial-sized chef's kitchen on the other side of the house?

On the desk there's a laptop and on the wall there's a fifty-five-inch TV, except I don't have cable, or Netflix, or Hulu, or even Prime, so why I bought the TV, I couldn't tell you.

If anyone saw me these days I'd get a label.

If I was lucky that label would be… eccentric. But more likely than not, they'd call me… sad.

And that would be accurate.

I am sad. I'm just not a hundred percent sure why.

Maybe for all the things I lost. For all the ways I've tried to make up to the people who matter. For all the things I'll never have—things that have nothing to do with the size of a TV or the number of bathrooms in a house I don't even really live in, or a wet bar in the oversized home office.

I feel sorry for that family who lost this house. I really do. Because at least they treated it like a *home*. At least it was loved.

I don't love it.

I kick off my shoes as I enter the office and pour myself four fingers of bourbon. I sit on the couch, facing the window that faces the front yard—visible because of the fancy landscape lighting—and think about the game that just ended.

Sometimes people ask me why I do this. Why I make up these games. Why I fuck with so many lives. And I say, *Why not?*

I take a sip of my drink, still staring out the window, and ask myself that question now.

I don't reply.

Days pass and there's no more communication with Augustine. But Alexander shows up at my office—dutifully—every day at lunch to give it another try.

I drop the blinds on the windows that face the hallway and I kiss him. We try to get used to it, to each other, but…

"I don't think this is gonna work."

That's what he says now.

"Me either," I say, placing my hand on his cheek and slipping my tongue into his mouth.

He's getting better at kissing at least. For her pleasure, not mine.

He gets me hard every day. Every time we do this, he gets me hard. Because even though I'm not gay, I do enjoy men. Not typically alone, without a woman, but the reach for me isn't as far as it is for him.

"We should tell her," he says, still kissing me back.

"So tell her," I say, placing my hand on his. He squeezes my cock a little harder. His breath quickens. I have a moment of hope that maybe… just maybe he's coming around to the idea.

But he's not. Because he backs away, shaking his head. "I can't. Not like this."

"Not like… what?"

"Just… fuck, I don't know what we're even doing."

"Well…" I laugh. But then I decide. I'm tired of it too. So I shrug. I knew it would never work. And say, "Fine."

"That's it? Just fine?"

"What should I say? I can't fucking *make* you enjoy me. She can't make you either. This whole fucking deal is stupid."

"Then why are you doing it?"

"You know why. I want that building, Alexander. All you gotta do is let me buy it from you and I'll go away. I swear on my fucking father's life, I'll disappear. I'll never talk to her again. Hell, I don't want this any more than you do."

"But you'd take her," he says. Not a question.

"Sure." I shrug. "I still love her. But she's married to you, so… that's the end of that."

"She's going to divorce me," he says. "There's no way we make it past this… bullshit. So this…" He pans his hands wide. "This *arrangement* is the only way I keep her."

"Dude, what do you want me to say? I'm not gonna steal her from you. I'm not that guy anymore."

"But you'll take her after I'm gone, won't you?"

"I don't—"

"Fuck you," Alexander says. "Fuck you. Don't lie."

"She doesn't want me either. She wants us both. I can't give her you. You can't give her me. So just sell me the fucking building and make it all go away."

He inhales. Exhales. "It's not in my name or I would've."

Figures.

I walk over to the credenza in front of my office window, pour myself a drink—I do not offer one to Alexander—and say, "So… see you tomorrow?"

He pauses. Takes a moment to think about tomorrow. I sip my drink and wait him out.

None of this is the point.

He leaves without answering.

Dreams are unreliable things.

That's how I got here.

I had a dream.

It involves a building with a revolving door. Which I have always thought clever and ironic because you had to walk through a dose of reality to enter the dream inside the club.

It involves a bar called the Black Room and a restaurant called the White Room and a grand lobby that hides the elevators to the basement behind the stairs to the second-floor landing. And up there is another elevator that takes you up into another world. And off to the side of that landing, there is another, smaller, even more private bar that looks out onto the grand lobby and bar down below.

I want to own this place. This dream world. This haven from the stress and expectations of the outside world. I want to go back there, but you know what they say.

You can't ever go home again.

What does that mean, anyway? Like… yeah. You can. Unless the fucking apocalypse happened and your home was blown up or taken over by zombies, you can definitely go back there. It might not be the same place it was when you left, but it's still home.

I could make it work.

I could get all the members back together.

There could be parties down in the basement again. There could be drinks in the bar again. There could be rooms upstairs again.

I could be happy.

If Augustine would just sell me the building I could get all this back.

I could.

Two weeks ago. That's when I found out she and Alexander owned the building the club used to be in. Two weeks ago I was ready to fuck her over. Ready to do anything, everything, to get what I wanted.

So I called Alexander. Not her, him. And not because I'm sexist and I think the man is in charge of shit like this, either. I just didn't want to talk to her.

And I asked him stuff. Like… "Hey, what's going on with the building? What are you gonna turn it into? Ever think about selling it?"

And he said, "I'll have Augustine call you."

So she did.

And that conversation was something I'd imagined in the past and was not what I wanted to hear now, in the present.

It went like this.

"I hear you're interested in purchasing the Turning Point building."

"Yes. Sell it to me. You're not doing anything with it. It's been sitting empty for over a year now. Let me have it. I'll pay you. Cash. Fair market value."

"I don't need money. Alexander is wealthy, we have more money than we need."

Right then I knew. Because people who don't need money want things you don't typically want to give up.

"Then what's the price?" I asked.

"You."

Because of course it is.

"The life I've built—*we've built*—" which is a dig at me, because that we means him, "=--is dying, Jordan," she said. "It's dead, actually."

"So?"

"I'd like to revive it. We had something good once. Better than good, ya know?"

"I mean, what do you want me to say? It's not me. I'm not the problem here. You two are the problem. Just sell me the building and you can have what you want."

"But… it's *not* what I want. Well, I do want this. OK? I do. But not *like* this. Not like this. I need *you*, Jordan."

"I think that defeats the purpose of being married, Augustine."

"No, you misunderstand," she said. "It's just so complicated now. It didn't used to be like that, remember? I don't just need him. Or you. I need you *both*."

And there it was. The price I'd have to pay.

CHAPTER TWO

Two weeks ago that same day, I first called Alexander and have my first sit down with them.

"So what do you think about all this?"

This is my first question to Alexander.

And it's funny, ya know. When I first found out they owned the building I was ready to play dirty with these two to get what I want, but this… it isn't the kind of dirty I've been imagining.

Alexander is sitting across from me. Actually, both of them are sitting across from me. It's a small, round table on the Tea Room patio. They are facing the street and I am facing my building. Because Turning Point is right next door.

My friend Chella owns the Tea Room. She's not here. Still on maternity leave after having her first child with Smith Baldwin, who, along with Elias Bricman and Quin Foster, was one of the former Turning Point owners.

I should've bought it back then. Why the fuck didn't I buy it back then?

Alexander looks at his wife. Smiles. It's a small smile. And says, "I'll do anything for her."

I want to roll my eyes. The thing no one ever understood about what happened between us almost eight years ago now was that Augustine was just as guilty as anyone. Yeah, I was the asshole. I'll take that responsibility. But she wanted all of it. She wanted everything I was doing. And this meeting right now just proves it.

"So..." I start. But what do you say when a married couple comes to you with something like this?

"So I want us to try, Jordan," Augustine says. "Just... give it a try. Like the old days."

"It didn't work." I laugh. "We did try. And it didn't work."

"We're different now," Augustine says. "More mature. We've tried things, learned things about ourselves, and..." She falters for words. Almost sighs with resignation. "And we love each other."

I raise one eyebrow at Alexander. "He doesn't love me."

"He could," Augustine insists.

"I don't love him," I say. "I'm not sure I even like him."

Augustine purses her lips. "Since when do you need to like someone to fuck them?"

"OK," I say. "So this is a temporary fantasy? You want a game? Is that what I'm hearing? You want me to arrange a game for you, only I'm one of the players?"

"Not a game," she corrects, eyes darting quickly over to Alexander, then just as quickly back at me. Like she didn't want me to see that. "I want us to try to make something real. Something that might last."

"Last?" She's crazy. "He's not into it, Augustine. All three of us know this. He's. Not. Interested."

Augustine looks at her husband. He's already looking at her. He says, "I'm interested."

"You're lying," I say. "Just tell her, Alexander. Just tell her no, for fuck's sake. Just sell me the building and I'll go away. It's that fucking simple. And hey," I say, directing my gaze to Augustine now. "I'll play your game for a while too. I don't care. I'll fuck you both. How long do you need to get it out of your system? A week? Two? A month? I can do that. I'll show up and give you both a good time. Just sell me the fucking building."

"Why do you need that building?" she snaps.

"Why do you need me to save your marriage?" I snap back.

"Keep your voices down," Alexander says, glaring at us both. "We're in public, for fuck's sake."

"We're at the Tea Room," I growl at him. "Which is pretty much filled with ex-club members right now. And you know why we all hang out at the goddamned Tea Room? It's because we all want the fucking club back. So we come here to see Chella. Maybe get a glimpse of Smith, or Bric, or Quin. Stare at that fucking revolving door that never revolves anymore, and wonder if we'll ever find another place that feels like home again. So don't get self-righteous on me, Alexander. We're here having this conversation because you're too weak to tell your wife no."

Augustine pushes a piece of long, dark hair away from her eyes and tucks it behind her ear. "This is my offer. You need something from me? Well, I need something from you too. It's up to you now."

She stands up, places her paper napkin on top of her uneaten cupcake, turns on her heel, and walks away.

I watch her hail a cab—and isn't that her luck? That one is passing by right at this moment?—get in and disappear.

Then I turn back to Alexander and say, "Just let her leave you. Why do you put up with this shit?"

He doesn't answer me. Just sits there and sips his coffee. A waitress comes by and he taps her arm as she passes, asking for a take-out container. She returns a few minutes later—neither of us have spoken in that silence—and he carefully places Augustine's cupcake inside the yellow box and ties the little black ribbon around it.

Then he stands, forces a smile, and says, "Let me know what time you have lunch tomorrow. I'll stop by and see if we can make this work."

I just stare at him as he leaves. He doesn't take a cab. His Land Rover is parked at the curb. He just drives away.

And that's what we've been doing for the past two weeks.

He didn't even want to touch me that first day. In fact, it took him four days to touch me, and then it was just a hand on my arm. Feeling the muscles underneath my button-down shirt. But he couldn't look at me.

And look, maybe we weren't *great* back in LA when we did this the first time. But it was a helluva lot better than this. At least he was sorta into it before.

Now, he's only here for his wife.

The next day I took off my shirt as he watched. This is all happening in my office, by the way. People outside. My fucking father down the hall. But Alexander didn't want to go to a hotel room. Or their house. Or my house. So… whatever.

This dude is never going to let me fuck him, because this whole lunchtime sexy shit? It's kinda hot, right? Like… people are even just a little bit into someone find this exciting and... dangerous. So yeah. This is never gonna work.

Today is Saturday. The first Saturday I figured we'd take the day off—regroup—meet back up on Monday. But he called me that morning and said he'd be at my office for lunch. But when I got to the lobby, I saw both of them waiting for me.

I raised my eyebrows at Augustine and she just said, "I want to watch."

So that's what's she's been doing. Not every day. But twice a week so far.

Yesterday went better than usual, so maybe she figures today is our day?

She's dreaming. Alexander just isn't into it.

"We're going somewhere," Augustine says as I approach them in the lobby. "You don't really have to work today, do you?"

"I guess not," I say, glancing at Alexander. He's wearing board shorts, a white t-shirt, and sneakers.

"You'll need to go home and change," Alexander says, eyeballing me eyeballing him.

"We'll follow you. Alexander can drive us."

"Follow me?" I'm not following.

"To your house," Augustine says. "To change."

I stew about this turn of events the whole way over to my place. How she just assumes control over us. And yeah, I've been in plenty of threesomes where I'm dude number two and take orders, but I've never taken orders from the woman.

Sexist? Maybe. But I'm not one of those submissive guys.

Maybe Alexander is. Maybe he's OK putting up with her dominance. But I'm not. And right now—as I wait for the gate of my ridiculous seven-million-dollar monstrosity to open, glancing back at them in my rear-view mirror—I'm kinda pissed off.

I pull forward when the gate is fully open, park in my usual spot in front of the carriage house, and get out just as Alexander turns off his engine.

Augustine is already getting out, looking up at the house with wide eyes. "You live here?"

I nod. "Yup."

"Why?" She laughs.

"Because I liquidated all my assets to buy my fucking club back." It comes out like venom. I'm not proud of that because I hate letting people in on my feelings, but she's pissing me off.

"Show me around," Augustine says, pretending that everything is cool.

"No," I say, walking around to the front door. I don't know why I always enter at the front door since I park in back, but I do. Maybe because the office is near the front door and I just want to pretend the rest of the house doesn't exist.

"Holy shit," Augustine says as we enter into the two-story foyer. "That's some chandelier."

I look up at it, probably for the first time in months, and notice there's still a camera bulb up there from when I made Ixion play a game here with Evangeline Rolaine.

Augustine walks forward into the long hallway that runs the length of the house. But I say, "There's nothing to see here. The place is empty except for the office."

She doesn't seem to care. Because she disappears around a corner, her fingertips tracing the wall as the last thing to fade away as she goes off to explore.

"So where are we going?" I ask Alexander. He's walked into the ballroom and is looking up at the intricate design on the coffered ceiling. "So I know what to wear," I add, when he doesn't answer me.

"Wear what I'm wearing," he replies back. Like it's an afterthought.

"I don't own cargo shorts," I say.

"Wear whatever the fuck you want," he snaps.

OK.

I go into the office, start rummaging through the portable clothes rack that holds about a hundred and fifty thousand dollars in suits, and find a t-shirt.

It's plain, dark blue, and brand new with tags. Which I rip off with my teeth and spit into the trash can by the desk.

I take off my suit coat, unbutton my shirt, take it off, and when I turn around, arms already in the sleeves of the t-shirt, Alexander is watching me.

I smile at him. "You can watch if you want. I don't care."

He looks away, wanders out of view, and I go rummage though the built-in drawers that now hold all my foldable clothes instead of office supplies.

I have a pair of sweat shorts that I usually wear to the gym. They'll do, so I slip those on.

This time when I turn around, Augustine is watching me. She smiles. "What is this place?"

"My house," I deadpan.

"Why are you living like this?"

"I told you, I'm liquidating. So I can pay you cash for the building when you finally sell it to me. No bank is gonna give me a loan to open a sex club."

"Why don't you have furniture?"

"Because it's dumb."

She laughs. "You know, you were always a weird guy, Jordan. But this… this is a whole new level of strange. Just live at the Four Seasons."

"Why would I pay for a hotel room at the Four Seasons when I have this?"

"Because at least you'd have the appearance of being normal. This is over the top. You do realize that, right?"

I shrug and go looking for sneakers. Find them and sit on the edge of the desk as I slip them on and tie the laces. "So where we going today?" I ask.

"Up to the river."

"What river?"

"Poudre. We have a cabin up there now. It's nice. Quiet. Bring a change of clothes too. We're staying overnight."

I feel obligated to object, but it actually sounds nice. So I don't. Just pack up a duffel bag and say, "OK, let's go."

The whole drive up to the Poudre River cabin I am lost in thought. It's not like there aren't a million thoughts to get lost in, either. So the hour-and-a-half drive is filled with silence because Augustine, who is sitting in the back, has her earbuds in. Alexander just drives. And so I just sit there wondering what the fuck is happening.

How did they get this way? Like… what happened to them back in LA that this is who they are now? Also… wow, I feel like I dodged a bullet. Because I could be driving this car and some other man could be sitting in the passenger seat next to me while my wife ignored both of us.

I almost feel sorry for the dude.

It's not like I ever hated Alexander. I didn't. I was jealous, of course. Because she chose him and not me. But he's older than us. So I guess I get why a twenty-three-year-old woman would choose a thirty-year-old man over a guy her own age. He had a career, and a house, and all that shit twenty-something women want.

I was in law school, so while it was a promising beginning he was well past that.

Choosing him was the right choice, I decide.

The cabin is just a small, two-room box made of logs. It's quaint and it has electricity and plumbing, so that's a plus. But this isn't really my idea of a weekend getaway in the mountains. I was picturing, you know, a five-thousand-square-foot custom log home.

"Is that disgust I see on your face, Jordan?"

I turn away from the cabin and stare at Augustine. She's standing in a beam of sunlight, her dark hair blowing slightly in the soft breeze. And for the first time I notice that she looks… older. Tired, maybe. Or defeated. That might be the word.

She's still pretty though. And every now and then she'll smile at something—it's not usually me, or Alexander—and she'll look young again.

"No," I say. "I'm fine."

"Good," she says. And then turns, walks up to the front door, unlocks it, and disappears inside.

Alexander is getting their bags from the back of the Land Rover and the hatch closes with a soft click as he walks past me.

He still hasn't said a word.

"What did you do?" I ask abruptly.

"What?" Alexander turns to look at me.

"What did you do to her? To make her like this?"

Alexander drops the bags on the ground next to him. One hand lifts his sunglasses up and places them on the top of his head. He stares at me.

He still looks good. I mean, he's what? Thirty-seven? Thirty-eight now? But he still looks good. Sandy blond hair. Blue eyes. Square jaw that doesn't have a regular date with a razor. And he's still very fit. He's tan too, even though they left LA a while ago. He looks like a guy who drives a Land Rover. Not because it's a hundred-thousand-dollar status symbol either, but because he needs it to get places other cars can't go.

"You did this to her," Alexander says.

"No," I say, shaking my head. "This has nothing to do with me."

"Then why are we here, Jordan? Hmm? God, you are so fucking stupid sometimes. Do you ever look around and just… see what's happening? Or do you like it in the dark?"

I don't answer, since I figure that was rhetorical.

So he picks up the bags, turns away, and goes inside.

CHAPTER THREE

I spend that entire afternoon still wondering what the fuck we're doing. Augustine is morose, Alexander is quiet, and I'm just… confused.

At one point Alexander says he's going to drive to the small store we passed on the way in and pick up some food. I try to go with him, but he says, "No. I want to be alone."

OK.

So now it's me, still confused, and Augustine, still morose.

I sit on the couch wishing I'd asked Alexander to pick up some alcohol. Because I really feel like getting drunk.

"Because I want you to watch us," Augustine says out of nowhere.

"What?"

"Have sex," she explains. "I want you to watch us." She looks me in the eyes. "Then tell us what you see."

I have a million things to say in reply. Like so many words popping into my head in this moment, it's impossible to choose one direction. So I say nothing.

"Will you do that? Will you give us an honest assessment?"

"Augustine… I don't know what you're looking for, but Alexander clearly isn't into this. OK? He doesn't like men. We've always known that. He doesn't want me watching you two fuck. And he certainly doesn't want my opinion on his goddamned performance."

"You're wrong," she says.

"Look, I don't know what happened to you two, but this has nothing to do with me."

"Wrong again."

I want to fucking choke her right now. Like… I have no clue what I ever saw in this woman, because I see nothing attractive about her now. In fact, her dismissive attitude towards Alexander is kinda pissing me off.

"Maybe I don't really need that building," I say.

"Maybe not."

"What the fuck do you want?"

"I told you. Watch us. Tell us what you see."

"I don't understand."

"There's no hidden meaning, Jordan. No agenda here. Just… watch us. And tell us what you see. How many times do I have to repeat myself before you hear what I'm saying?"

I draw in a deep breath. Hold it. Let it out. And say, "Fine. But I want a deadline. I want a firm date on when this can be over and you'll sell me the building. Because I'm not fucking around forever, OK? I'm not gonna let you own me the way you own him. Fuck that. Give me a *date*."

She closes her eyes. Just a slightly exaggerated blink. Then opens them and says, "Two months."

"Fuck you." I laugh. "No. I'm gonna fucking hitchhike back to civilization right now if you think I'm gonna put up with this bullshit for two months."

"One month."

"No," I say. Because I'm beginning to understand that she needs me more than I need her. She's holding this building over my head, but only because that's the thing she has that I need. And if I walk away from the building, I walk away from her.

Funny. How you can go eight years feeling like a rejected loser and then suddenly figure out your perception was entirely wrong.

"One week," I say.

"You know that's not enough time."

"Time for what?"

"To get us all on the same page?"

"For a threesome? Jesus, Augustine, let's just do it now. He's obviously doing whatever you tell him. Let's just fuck and get it over with."

"No, that's not what I'm looking for. I don't need a third partner to fuck, Jordan. I could get almost anyone to do that. I want you. With us."

"I'm here," I say.

"No. With. Us."

"Like…" I laugh. "In a *relationship*?"

"Yes, in a relationship. But a real one. And that takes time."

"He's not gonna share you with me, Augustine."

"No, he's not. Unless he loves you too. Then it's the three of us sharing each other."

"You're insane. He's never gonna come around."

"He's already *around*," she snaps. "It's you who's not on board. You're the one holding this up. You're the one fighting it. You know we're good together. And you know this because we've been together before."

"Yeah, once. And he wasn't into it."

"You're wrong, as usual. It was me who wanted you out. Not him."

"Liar." I laugh. "That's not true and you know it."

"Ask him."

"I don't trust him to tell the truth. He's your little puppet."

"God," she says, shaking her head. "You're so stupid for being so smart. He was the one who loved you, Jordan. Not me. He's the one who wanted a divorce, not me. He's the one who made us come back here. And you're the one he wants."

I get up and leave at that point. A guy can only take so many lies in the same sentence. Why is she saying those things? I was there. I know what happened. And nothing of what she just said was even remotely true. Not the part about them. I have no clue what drove them apart. Well, I have some clue. It wasn't Alexander's love for me.

So I end up outside sitting on a rock by the river, throwing stones into the water to scare away the tiny minnows near the shore.

Alexander comes back some time later. When I look over my shoulder at him, he's staring at me as he unloads bags from the back.

He's got his hands full, already heading to the door, when he looks over his shoulder and says, "You should come inside now."

I wait a little bit, trying to sort through my confusion. But eventually I get up, brush off the dirt, and go back in. Because I'm out of here. I'm gonna ask them to take me back to Fort Collins and drop me off and I'll rent a car from there, or have someone come pick me up, because this is all bullshit.

I open the door, ready to say all that, and find them kissing in the kitchen.

His hand is between her legs, rubbing against her clit. Her thigh is between his, pressing up against his cock. His other hand grips her breast and squeezes. Then it's sliding up her chest, and resting on her throat, and she opens her mouth as her head tips back, and waits for him to follow her lead.

Their kiss is long, and passionate, and they breathe heavy and fast.

And even though this is my job, a job I said I wouldn't do, I can't help it.

I watch.

She's wearing a white tank t-shirt. Alexander grabs the collar and pulls down, taking her bra with the shirt, so her breasts are lifted up by the bunched-up fabric beneath them, popping out of her shirt.

He's whispering something in her ear now. Something low. Something I strain to hear, but can't. Almost move closer because I'm so curious. What does he say to her? Is it the same thing every time? Something stupid and dirty like, "Do you want my cock inside you?" Something like that?

Or maybe… maybe it's something kinda sweet. Something like, "I ache for you."

Augustine whines, her head nodding, eyes still closed. "Yes," she squeaks out. "Yes," she whispers again.

My guess is… it's not sweet.

Alexander backs up, letting his hand drop from her throat as he leads her past me—grinning, but just briefly—like he's showing me a secret. Until they're standing in front of the couch.

He leans into her ear and whispers again. This time Augustine's eyes are open as she nods, her face flushed, beads of sweat on her temple making her hair glisten, biting her lip…

God, what is he saying? Because it's driving her crazy with lust.

He places a hand on her shoulder and urges her to sit on the couch in front of him. For a second I think I know where this is going, but I'm wrong. Because she lifts her legs up, bending her knees and spreading herself wide. Her skirt riding up her legs, giving him total access.

Alexander snaps her legs closed with a firm grip on both knees, then in one quick, rushed movement, he's got her panties down at her ankles. A moment later they're flying across the room in my direction.

His gaze follows them, then his eyes find mine. "Stay right there," he says. "She's mine."

OK. I almost laugh. I mean, clearly she's *not* or I wouldn't be here.

But if he notices my smirk, he doesn't care. And I'm not going to interfere anyway. She told me to watch, so fuck it. I'll watch.

I lean against the kitchen island about twenty feet away from them, cross my arms, and just *observe.*

He's dominant now and while she's not quite submissive, she's not in charge anymore either.

Alexander drops to his knees, spreads her open again, and starts kissing her leg, starting mid-calf and working his way up. He pauses at her knee, biting the soft flesh on the underside. This makes her breathe heavy and wiggle a little as she squeaks out pointless protests. Then he moves on, nipping and kissing the inside of her thigh. One finger is already inside her, his thumb massaging her clit. I can see that she's wet. His finger is slick with her lust.

But instead of eating her pussy, he pushes her shirt up one-handed and whispers, "Take it off," just loud enough for me to hear.

Against my better judgement, I move closer to hear him better. He's a talker and I find talking to be a powerful stimulant… especially when I'm just observing.

It's been a long time since I just got to watch. When the club was open it was a regular thing. Just another part of my sex life. And it was easy to get lost in someone else's fantasy. I mean… we—the players—were all that place contained. So they put on a show, or I put on a show, and they watched me, or I watched them and it was… normal.

Just another move in the game.

I don't think they could know that though. How could they? So this is how they play too. Two people on exhibit.

I like it.

There's a chair about four feet away from them, so I take a seat, my legs open, my hand on my cock. It's not hard, but it's growing underneath the loose fabric of my sweat shorts.

Augustine has her shirt and bra off now. Her breasts are just as perfect as I remember them. Better, maybe. Like the years have only added to her beauty. She's not wearing make-up today, but she looks radiant and fresh now. So different then she was just a few hours ago when we arrived.

It's him, I realize. He's making her look this way.

It's not jealousy I feel in this moment of realization, it's something else. Like I've missed something. Or maybe… missed *out* on something.

His fingers are strumming her clit. Short, quick back-and-forth movements. And then he's got two fingers inside her, pumping her hard. She squirts liquid up into the air and Alexander smiles. Like he just won a prize.

Her fingernails are digging into his upper arms like a vice. Gripping him like she never wants to let go.

"You're a good girl, Mrs. Bartos," Alexander croons.

"Yes," she squeaks. "I'm very good." Then she grabs his hair with both hands and stares into his eyes. "I'm good," she insists. "I am."

Then I have this… this moment of recognition. Augustine and the little begging she liked to do and it makes me feel, once again, like I've been missing something.

Because I forgot about that. I'd forgotten all her little tells. All the little ways she'd let us know she was having a good time, or that she wanted more, or… she's just *enjoying* herself. All the small things she'd say or the words she'd use. So that we knew, whatever it was we were doing, she liked it. And we should keep going.

"I know," he says, one finger stroking her cheek as he continues to pump two fingers inside her.

Her back bucks up. Spine arching like she's about to come. She bites her lip and he kisses it, whispering something inaudible. I lean forward, wanting to catch the words, but they escape into the air and float away.

Alexander takes her hand and places it over his cock. She unbuttons his shorts with nimble fingers and pulls him out, her hand automatically wrapping around his long, thick shaft.

He's always had a nice cock, now that I think about it.

But then she's done stroking and places him near her entrance.

"What do you want?" Alexander asks her. Staring intently down into her eyes.

She stares back, speechless now, like she's lost in the moment. Like she's somewhere else and she's trying to find her way back.

And I feel like saying, *She wants you to fuck her, dude. Obviously.*

But she says it for me. "Do it. Do it, *please*."

He leans back, his legs open, sitting on the floor in front of her. "Are you sure?" he asks, tilting his head to the side a little. Grinning.

"Yes, yes!" she whines. Scooting her ass forward until it's hanging off the edge of the couch cushion.

He moves his hips forward, reaching for her as it bumps up against her pussy, and I find myself holding my breath as I wait for him to enter her. To fuck her. To make her scream.

But he doesn't. "This," he says, positioning the tip of his cock against her swollen clit.

"Yes, yes," she repeats. Only this time it's just small sounds mixed with breath.

He presses it up against her wet flesh and she moans. Then he flicks it back and forth and Augustine goes wild. Her mouth clamps shut as she hums out something incoherent.

He does it again and she hisses through her teeth. Then again, and she's moaning. He's flicking the tip of his dick back and forth across her clit, so fast it blurs and a moment later she…

Explodes.

Literally squirts up in the air, moans and screams coming out of her mouth, and I can only assume she's coming. But it goes on and on and on. And she's begging him now, not to fuck her, but not to stop.

But he does stop.

And I swear to God, I think she just has one continuous orgasm that lasted five minutes at least.

She is exhausted. Her thighs are trembling as she holds her legs open for him. Sweat is pouring down her face. She is flushed pink from her cheeks to her belly.

She is spent.

And he never even put his cock inside her.

Their foreplay was so well… choreographed I suddenly feel like an unwelcome outsider. Like… a voyeur of the worst kind.

The kind who invades someone's privacy.

The kind who steals little secrets and moments to use for himself later when he… when he has no more fantasies of his own and needs something to make him feel…

Jesus, Jordan. Get a fucking grip.

Alexander lets out a laugh and then climbs up onto the couch, pulling her close to him as he closes her legs and holds her tight.

She melts. Melds her body into his, and they become one.

It occurs to me then how much of them I've missed these past several years. How well they know each other. How she kept the little things that made her… *her*. And he kept the little things that made him… him. And then they rearranged them. Scattered them all around and scrambled them all up like a game of memory, waiting to be matched back up again in a new way.

Yeah, they grew apart, but they've grown together too.

And I missed it.

They take a shower after that and I go back outside and sit by the river. Reliving their sex over and over again in my head. Unsure how I feel about it. Unsure what it was, actually. Which is dumb. Because it's just… just two people who've been together for a very long time doing things they've done a million times before.

It just bothers me though. How well they know each other. How each one knows just what to do. How to do it. When to do it.

Why the fuck do they need me? I mean, shit, if I had that on film like the old days…

I shake that thought away by shaking my head.

That's not how I remember sex with Augustine and Alexander. And we've fucked her together plenty of times back in the day.

I remember it as… just… I dunno. Blind lust. Hard, thumping heart beats and sweaty bodies all twisted up in sheets. It was intimate, but not like this. More desperation and less devotion. It was urgent and reckless.

Nothing they did in there was anything less than careful.

So again… why am I here?

I am no closer to that answer than I was before I watched them.

A little while later Augustine comes outside, the screen door of the cabin smacking against the door frame as the spring swings it closed. She's wearing a loose turquoise tank top and a pair of cut-off shorts, looking like the girl I left behind and not the one who brought me here today.

She sits down next to me, smelling of soap, leans back, propped up with palms flat on the rock, and says, "So… what'd we do wrong?"

I laugh. "What the fuck are you talking about? I felt like I was watching porn."

I look at her and find her looking at me with squinted eyes. "You didn't even notice?"

"Notice what? That he didn't fuck you? Didn't look like you needed it, Augustine."

"He didn't come."

"Oh," I say, thinking about that. "I guess I didn't notice. I was too busy looking at you."

"Right? I mean, that's why it took me so long to notice too! But he doesn't come, Jordan."

"What do you mean? Like ever?"

"Well, he comes when he masturbates. But I haven't been able to make him come in almost a year."

"Are you fucking serious? But he gets hard. His cock is fucking huge."

"I know. There's no problem in that area. He just… I just…" She winces and sighs. Like she knows what she needs to say, she's just unwilling to say it.

"You don't turn him on?" I ask.

She shakes her head. "No. That's not it."

"Then what?"

"I dunno. He's just…" She looks me in the eyes. "He wants more than me. He won't leave me. I don't want to leave him. But… he wants you. Here with us."

I laugh. So loud. "Come on."

"I mean it."

"No. Whatever your problem is, that's not it. He can't even kiss me without wanting to walk out, Augustine. This makes no sense."

"I've asked him about that. Why he doesn't just… you know. With you."

"What's he say?"

"He says… he says you don't want him the same way so he… can't. He's fucking weird, OK? I dunno. He's just fucking weird."

"But you love him."

"He's the only guy for me, Jordan."

Which, I'm not going to lie, fucking hurts to hear. Even if it can't be true. I mean, she is here with *me*, right? Asking *me* to join *them*. But I keep my mouth shut because it's not the time or the place for that kind of self-absorbed bullshit. She's asking me for help. She wants me to save her marriage. And I want her to sell me that stupid building.

This is a game.

She wants me to put together a game for her, only I'm the one of the playing pieces.

"Three weeks," she says. "We didn't finish our negotiation. But three weeks, OK? And if we can't fix this in three weeks I'll sell you the building and Alex and I will get out of your life." She takes a deep breath and extends her hand. "Deal?"

But there's something behind her words. Something I recognize, just barely. Something nagging at the back of my mind. A little itch that says… *Pay attention. This contract has small print somewhere. Print so tiny you can't even see it.*

It's the lawyer in me. The instincts I've honed over the last several years in court. The thing inside that recognizes the details not being negotiated.

I shake her hand anyway.

Partly because OK, I can handle three weeks of kink with two people I've already shared a shitload of kink with. And partly because that building is as good as mine.

But mostly because this *wasn't* how it was.

We used to be good together. They used to be good together.

"What happened?" I ask her.

"What do you mean?"

"I mean back when we were all together. You, me, Ixion, Alexander… it was fun, right?"

She looks sad for a moment. Like we're remembering two completely different things.

But it was good. It was good…

CHAPTER FOUR

LA was unbearably hot that summer. I was on break from law school. Ixion and Augustine were working together by that time. Making film shorts and shit you do after film school. Alexander was the money. He had some consultant gig for the film industry.

It was his loft we all lived in. The AC was broken, I remember that because it was motherfucking hot. He has this giant fan. Like one of those industrial wind machine things you see in gyms. It was so loud we'd have the TV on full blast and still couldn't hear it but we couldn't turn it off.

I don't even remember why the AC was broken. Maybe it was a scheduling thing. Couldn't get anyone out or something. Because it was fixed later, when things were just getting ready to cool down.

But the passion we had that summer kinda faded with the heat. It's like we needed to sweat the lust out of us.

Everything was uncomfortable. The sex, the sleep, hell, even the showers. Because you'd get out and the humidity would hit you like a wet blanket.

Sometimes even Ixion was there, watching, as usual. He did join in once or twice, but not that summer. He just watched.

It was me, and Alexander, and Augustine. Weeks and weeks of *us*.

What happened to him? I wonder.

He never had a problem kissing me back then. It didn't take much to make him hard. And even though neither of us was looking for a man—we were just part of the triangle—we sure as fuck had some fun. Even when Augustine wasn't there a few times.

And she was… Jesus. She was the girl who could swing a bat, play pool, ride a motorcycle, and look hot doing it.

I let out a small laugh, which makes Augustine look over at me, my question still hanging in the air between us.

"You were different back then," I say.

"What do you mean?"

"Just…" I look at her and all the tomboy is gone now. She's a woman. No trace of that girl. And even though she's wearing shorts and a tank top—pretty much what she wore every day back then too—it's not the same. "You're not the same."

"Explain," she says. "Because I think I am. Inside, anyway, I am."

"Maybe," I say. "But that look in your eyes—it's gone now."

"What look?"

"The wild, ya know. The dare. The don't-fuck-with-me. It's gone. You're…" I shrug. "His *wife* now."

She makes a face. You know what it means when you see it, but I'm not sure there's a word for it. It's an eye roll, but more. Something in between disgust and contempt that comes out as a huff of air between barely parted lips.

"You wanna know what's different?" I ask.

She looks at me and nods.

"It's Ixion."

She huffs again, but this time it comes with a very small smile. "No. He was never involved in this."

"I know, but he told me something a few months back. When he was mad at me. He said, 'I was the glue.' And I didn't even really understand what he meant, ya know. But I've thought about that a lot since then and I think he's right. He was the glue. It wasn't me. It wasn't Alexander. It was him."

"I've tried to talk to him, he's not interested."

"I know, but that's because he's finally happy. He let the past go. He's moved on and I'm glad for that. So leave him alone. Don't bring him into this."

She sighs. Scratches her neck. Runs her fingers through her hair. "I couldn't even if I wanted to. I told you, he won't speak to me."

"You know it wasn't him, right? You do know it was me."

"I know," she says softly. "I've let it all go, Jordan. I'm over it. I just… I just want… I dunno."

"You want the past back, Augustine. And that's not possible. I mean, I'll play your little game, but it's not going to matter. None of this can save your marriage if that's what you think. If I were you, I'd accept what Alexander gives you with gratitude."

"The fuck?"

I shrug. "He looked like he was having fun in there. So what's the problem?"

"The problem is… the problem *is*…" Her eyes dart back and forth, like she's not sure what to say. "The problem is… if he refuses to come I'll never get pregnant."

"Whoa," I say. "If you think I'm giving the two of you a fucking kid, you can just fuck off right now. I'm not doing it."

"That's not what I said. And anyway, that's not the plan."

"The plan?" I say. Because that itch is back. The one telling me to look a little closer at the fine print. "What is the fucking plan? Alexander and I fuck around and what? He suddenly realizes he loves you and wants to stay?"

"He wants you. He's the one who wants the past back, not me. I'm doing this for him."

"Well, that's funny. He said the same thing about you. So looks like none of us know what the fuck is going on. Maybe you should go back inside and figure that out, Augustine. Because I'm not some magic oracle with all the answers. I'm a fucking Pandora's Box. So you'd better be very fucking careful if you decide to open me up."

She just stares at me. Eyebrows narrowed. Questioning. Lots of questions running through her mind about what I just said.

And then—because I know her, because I know she won't get up and leave—I get up and leave instead. I walk downstream, following the river.

And I don't even look back.

The first time I met Augustine she and Ixion were sharing an apartment down the street from UCLA. It was a total shithole, but it was home. I used to come down from Stanford for spring break while I was in undergrad. At first to just kick it with Ix. But then, for both of them.

The first time we ever fucked Alexander wasn't there. It was just the three of us. I think she might've known Alexander at that time, but they weren't a thing yet.

She and I… well, it was lust at first sight. I was fucking her in the bathroom two hours later. We were all pretty drunk and Ixion had some people over, so he didn't notice we were missing right away. I don't know why I was fucking her in the bathroom. But it was fucking hot. I had her propped up on the sink, one leg raised in the air, my cock plunging inside her, disappearing, then pulling back out, slick and shiny with her desire. She was digging her nails into my shoulders the same way she was digging into Alexander's inside.

We both heard Ixion calling for us. People had left, he was suddenly aware we were gone. And the door wasn't locked so he walked right in. Innocent mistake? Probably not. But no one cared. He just walked up to us, put his hands on her face, and kissed her mouth.

And then I joined in.

So maybe we were drunk. But we did it again a few more times before Ix figured out this was bad news for the working relationship they were forging. He backed away, slowly, quietly and without drama.

And then it was just me and her. Ix would watch. That was always his thing. Even after Alexander joined us, he'd watch.

But after we graduated and I moved down to LA for law school… that's when shit got serious. That's when I moved in with them.

That's what she's trying to recreate with this little reunion.

When I go back to the cabin it's dark. But they've got lights on inside and it looks cozy and shit, ya know? Like…

if I didn't know better I'd think it was pretty fucking normal. Maybe even perfect.

But when I open the door and walk inside Augustine is on the couch—the same place where Alexander fucked her earlier—reading a book. And Alexander is sitting at the kitchen table, talking business on his cell phone. He looks at me, nods his head, and never breaks his conversation.

Augustine just turns a page in her book. She's got her glasses on looking like a sexy nerd. Which used to make me want to fuck her when she wore that look back in LA.

I flop into the chair opposite. The same one I was sitting in, watching her get fucked.

Or fingered, as it was. Because Alexander never did fuck her, did he?

"What are you reading?" I ask.

"Required stuff," she says, taking her glasses off so she can see me properly.

"Required for what?"

"I'm in grad school. Just online stuff. Getting an MFA."

I laugh, I can't help it.

"What?" she snaps.

"Are you that bored with your life that you need grad school to keep you busy?"

Her eyes dart over my shoulder and when I look, Alexander has finished his phone call and is standing behind me. "I'm not bored," she says.

But she's not talking to me. She's talking to him.

"Want a drink?" Alexander asks me, ignoring her.

"Sure," I say. "I'll have what you're having."

I feel Alexander retreat back into the kitchen. Hear the sound of glassware and ice. Drinks being poured.

"I'm not bored," Augustine says again. This time she's talking to me.

"Well, why the fuck do you need an MFA then?"

"Maybe because I want to better myself?"

Alexander is standing in front of me then. Handing me a drink. I take the glass, take a sip, and shrug. "Whatever."

Alexander sits on the couch next to her. Hand immediately on her knee. And I don't think it's a possessive gesture, either. I think it's just habit.

"So," he says, looking at me. "What have you been up to, Jordan?"

And that's how we spend the rest of the evening. Small-talking.

I just… tell them. Because whatever, right? Who cares? And my business is safe. No feelings at all attached to my business. It's just me, and my dad, and the law firm.

And it's funny. Because we have an endless stream of small talk. We never stop small-talking. Some of it is memories. Most of it is catching up. But all of it is… *boring*.

Some time around midnight I say, "So where do I sleep?"

And Alexander says, "With us, of course."

There's only one bedroom in the cabin and it has a king-size bed. I'm on one side. Alexander is on the other. And Augustine is between us.

We are all naked.

We are all staring up at the ceiling like three strangers lying under a single white sheet.

We are all uncomfortable.

And then there's a shuffling. And movement. And a hand on my bare stomach that sends chills up my spine.

Her hand. Placed there. By his hand.

"You can have her tonight," he says. And then he turns over. Giving us permission and dismissing us in the same moment.

I turn my head. Just barely able to see her turn hers. Our eyes meet.

Then she turns over, hugs him, and sighs.

What the fuck am I doing here?

In the morning I'm the first one up. I'm not even sure it qualifies as morning, but I'm up. I can't take it anymore.

I have several viable escape plans.

One. Steal their car.

Two. Wake one of them up and ask for a ride into town.

Three. Walk away.

Aside from stealing the car, these are the same options I had yesterday.

Why. Am. I. Here?

"Why are you up?"

Alexander is standing in the doorway naked, hard, and sleepy.

"Dude, you wanna take me into FoCo and drop me off somewhere? Because otherwise I'm stealing your car."

He lets out a small laugh, walks into the kitchen, and starts making coffee.

I'm staring at his ass. It's pretty nice.

"Well?" I ask.

"What can I do to make you stay?"

"Why do you want me to stay? And don't say she wants me, OK? She says you want me. I feel very unwanted. So let's stop talking in circles."

"Obviously I'm looking to improve our relationship. And you're a part of that."

"How? It makes no sense, Alexander. I've been gone almost eight years now. We've all moved on."

"She hasn't."

"She says the same thing about you and you know what I see? I see two people making excuses and blaming me for their issues. If you don't love her—"

"I do love her," he says, interrupting me. "And she loves me."

"So what is the fucking problem?"

He turns to face me. Still naked. Still hard. Still very fucking distracting. "The problem is we are allowed to love more than one person in a lifetime."

"So you two… what? Swing and shit?"

"No," he says. "That's not what we mean. We want you, Jordan."

"I hear that. But I don't see it. And I don't feel it either."

"That's because it's taken us all these years to admit it and now that we have, now that we're here… well… we're afraid."

"Of?"

"It's a risk, right? Loving you. Together. There's always that doubt in your head, ya know. Maybe she'll love you more than me. Maybe you'll love her more than me. Maybe I'll love you more than her."

I… don't know what to say to that. So I just say the truth. "I don't love you guys."

Alexander leans back a little more. Hands gripping the counter. His cock still semi-hard. Eyes on mine. He says nothing.

"I mean…" I try to explain. "It was fun, ya know. It was hot." And then I laugh. "Literally, remember?"

He nods.

"But that's all it was. Just fun."

Alexander remains quiet. It's unsettling and I start to fidget, lean back against the counter, mirroring him.

"You know why it was hot?" he finally says.

"Yeah, the AC was broke."

"You remember why it was broke?"

"No," I say, shaking my head.

"People kept getting up on the roof that summer. Stealing the components out of the unit."

I laugh. "Oh, no shit? I don't remember that."

"No," he says. "You wouldn't because it wasn't your place, ya know? And I don't mean that like… like a being a dick or anything. I just mean, it wasn't your concern, right? It was mine. The reason it feels different now than it did then is because we were young. You, and Ix, and Augustine were all kids. And to you guys it was just fun. Just a phase, maybe. That's probably true for Ixion. He's moved on. Found his way."

I have to laugh at that. Because Ixion, fuck-up of the century, is being called the adult in this conversation.

"And now we're living this other life. One where August and I are married and having problems. One where you're adrift and having problems."

"Dude, I'm cool, man. I'm not having problems. For the most part things are going real well."

"For the most part, you say? Well, I'd have to disagree, Jordan. You're a top-notch lawyer now, sure. On your way to becoming one of the best defense litigators in the country. Gonna make full partner soon, probably. And yet… this side business you run. Your Game, I think it's called. And this business about the building. It's all, sadly, the same old, same old."

"You don't know me, so don't pretend like you do."

"I did know you. Pretty intimately."

"Well, clearly that's changed since you can't even bring yourself to kiss me properly anymore. I mean, what's the point of all this?" I throw up my hands. "You don't like me that way."

"You're right," he says. "I don't like you *that* way. But I do like you another way."

"What other way?"

"The way you are with us."

I huff some air. This is so stupid.

"I never walked out, Jordan. That was you. You hurt her—"

"I'm not that guy anymore."

"No, you're this guy now."

He's starting to piss me off. So I say, "Just go home. Just sell me the building and forget about me and take her home."

He's shaking his head before I'm even done talking. "She's not going home with me if this doesn't work. She's going somewhere, but I won't be with her."

"I can't save your fucking marriage, Alexander. I can't fix things for you."

"Our marriage is already over. That display we gave you last night… that's all that's left of us. Her getting off, me getting her off… that's it, that's all there is. And you know why, Jordan? Because it was never supposed to be the two of us. Believe me, we've been to a lot of fucking therapy trying to come to terms with why this won't work. And it took years for us to both admit that it was you who held us together."

Ixion's words echo in my head. When we fought last January. *I was the glue*, he'd said. "I'm not the glue," I say. "That isn't me. I was the one who broke us apart. I was—"

"We're here," Alexander says. "We're here, Jordan. Because it was you. And you can believe that or not. You can walk out and never look back if you want. Or…" He comes towards me in three quick steps, places his hand on the side of my neck, leans in and kisses my mouth. "Or," he whispers. "Or you can take off your fucking clothes, follow me into the bedroom, get into the bed with us, and try again."

He lets go of me and backs away.

Then he turns and disappears into the hallway.

I'm so stunned I just stand there for a moment. Feeling the touch of his lips on my lips for a minute or more. I place the tips of my fingers on them. Confused.

They murmur to each other in the bedroom.

Augustine's soft voice. His low response. Then silence.

We're allowed to love more than one person in a lifetime.

Are we? I mean, sure. We are. But more than one person at a time? How does that ever work?

That's why we had the club. That's why people went there. It wasn't love, it was just sex. There were rules, and clear expectations, and it was all… safe. We knew where we stood, we knew it was a fantasy. We knew the moment we stepped outside the door, reality took over.

And what Augustine and Alexander are telling me now is… is that it doesn't have to be that way.

Except it does.

Plural relationships are temporary arrangements. Things get in the way if they go on too long. Feelings grow unevenly, and expectations change unilaterally, and emotions run wild.

That's how it always ends.

We all know this. We've all lived this.

And it fucking hurt.

So why are we trying to relive that pain? Why would we want to?

They talk softly again. Probably wondering what I'm gonna do next.

And that's the problem.

I have no idea.

But as a lawyer I know the best defense is silence.

So I leave. I walk out. I make my way up to the main road and spend the next hour wondering if they'll come pick me up.

But they don't.

I get to the nearest store, call a car service in Fort Collins, and drink bitter black coffee as I wait for my ride home.

CHAPTER FIVE

I don't hear from them for the rest of the weekend but sure as shit, Alexander is at my office at noon on Monday.

Too bad I'm not there.

I'm in court. Well, sort of. I'm hiding at the courthouse.

Which kinda makes me feel stupid and childish, but fuck it. I don't know what to do with these two. And the funny thing is—the really ironic thing is... six months ago I'd have felt totally different.

I sit on a hallway bench, unwrap the avocado toast sandwich I just got from a lunch truck outside, and try to unpack my feelings at the same time.

My phone dings a text. I didn't answer Alexander's first text, so this is... yup. Augustine. It's an emoji making a mad face.

Six months ago... what was different about me?

Ixion, I decide. He and I were practically strangers. His life was a mess. And then I came along, hired him to help me with that game, we had it out (a few times) and even though I don't think we're exactly friends now, I'm pretty sure he'd bail me out of jail if I ever got arrested.

That's my benchmark for friendship. Can I call this person to bail me out?

I bailed him out before. But that's not why I think he'd be there for me. I just feel like we've turned a corner. He sees new me, not old me. Maybe he hasn't forgiven me. I did kinda fuck up his life. But he's at peace with it.

Maybe that's the most you can expect from your mistakes?

My phone rings. Alexander. I tab accept and say, "Yes."

"So you're done, I take it?"

"Yeah. I'm out. You two need to figure your shit out on your own. I can't be your glue."

"Cool," he says. "Fine. But…" He pauses. For too long.

"But what?"

"So you wanna go to dinner tonight?"

"Dude—"

"Just me, man. Not her."

I do meet up with him. Partly because I'm curious what he's up to. Like, is he wearing me down? Trying to make me change my mind? Is he using me to piss Augustine off? What is his fucking deal?

We meet at the restaurant, which is a small, intimate Italian place suitable for new couples. He gets there first, waiting for me outside in a slow, misty drizzle under a softly glowing yellow streetlamp.

He greets me with a smile, an outstretched hand—which I take, and shake—as he pulls me into a hug that comes with a firm clap on the back.

"I know you're avoiding me, so I appreciate the fact that you're here."

"Look, I'm not your fix, OK?"

"Consider that subject closed then."

"Closed?"

"Done."

"You're not here to talk me into it? Or tell me why I'm so important?"

"Let's go inside," he says, waving me towards the door.

And then he reaches ahead of me to pull the door open, like I'm his fucking date.

Inside all the arrangements were made by him, so he takes charge. And it's fucking weird because I feel like a woman.

How the fuck did I get here? I swear to God, none of this is my fault. I did nothing to ask for this bullshit. I've just been doing my thing these past several years. Moving on, and up, and a little bit out. I put things behind me for a reason and I have no interest in bringing them all front and center again.

We get to the table, which is an intimate two-seater with a fucking candle between us.

The waiter is smiling, happy to present us with the chef's specials, and then leaves us to get our drinks. Which Alexander orders for both of us.

"What the fuck are you doing?" I ask, once the waiter is gone.

"Showing you a nice time," he says, placing his napkin on his lap. "Just relax, Jordan. Enjoy yourself for once."

"I can't enjoy myself if I have to spend every waking minute wondering what your game is."

He smiles. Chuckles. "Ironic, isn't it? You, the game master, think I'm the one playing. I'm here for you, I thought I made that clear the other day."

"You want to date me?" I ask.

"Yes, Jordan," he says. "Yes. Now that Augustine knows you're not interested in her or the three of us, I feel like..." He shrugs. "I feel like we can start over."

"As lovers?" I laugh and it's not a chuckle. It's kinda loud.

"You're not attracted to me?"

I look him over. Alexander is a good-looking man. He's athletic. And if I remember correctly he's into horses. Like he plays polo or something like that. He's got a square jaw, piercing blue eyes, and sandy-blond hair cropped close on the sides and a little longer in the front. So every now and then—despite the fact that he's well-groomed—a strand or two will escape and fall over his forehead.

We're about the same height. Six two for me, maybe six one for him.

Both come from money, both well-educated, both...

"So what do you do now?" I ask. Because I realize I don't actually know anything about the guy. I didn't pay much attention to how he made money back in LA, I just knew it had something to do with the film industry.

"I run my family corporation. Which is a major arts endowment."

"So you're what? A professional board member?"

"You could say that."

The waiter appears with a bottle of Macallan 18, pours a healthy amount into our glasses, then leaves.

Alexander raises his and says, "To Denver. May this city bring us more than we had in LA."

"Sure," I say, "Whatever," taking a sip and pausing to enjoy the burn of an excellent eighteen-year-old Scotch.

He watches me, smiling. Making me feel self-conscious. It's been a long time since a man could put me on edge like this, but Alexander always was that man, wasn't he?

"I'm so tired of asking this question, but here goes. Why are we here?"

He shrugs. Puts his glass down. Slowly twirls it on the tablecloth with his fingers. "We could find another girl," he finally says.

"What?"

"Someone who isn't August, ya know? Someone new. No baggage. No expectations. Just… a fresh start."

I have to run all that in my head several times before I can accept he actually *said that.* That *those* words just came out of *his* mouth.

"I mean, we could try just us, ya know? But I don't think it would work."

I just blink at him. "What?"

"Jordan," he says, leaning forward. "I came here for you and I'm not leaving until I get you."

"What happened to the guy who didn't want to kiss me two weeks ago?"

"That's because…" He pauses. "That was Augustine's idea. This one is mine."

"You're in love with me?"

"With us, Jordan. I want a plural relationship, one with two men and one woman, but maybe I don't want that with August. She's…"

I wait for him to finish and when he doesn't I get impatient. "She's *what*?"

"Look," he says, holding up a hand. "All your reservations go back to how it ended with the two of you. It's not really about me, is it? So she's the one you're avoiding. I'm just trying to make this work."

"I don't understand how you got the impression—"

"You're living in a ten-thousand-square-foot house by yourself, Jordan. That's how. You spend your life playing games with people because you can't play one yourself. You feel guilty for who you were, so now you hide under the umbrella of friend to everyone. Just as long as they don't get too close, right? No one gets close to you. Not even Ixion. I talked to him, ya know? He told me what you've been up to. Trying to make up for past mistakes is exhausting. So why don't we pronounce you absolved and move on, huh? It would be so much less exhausting."

I just stare at him.

He waits, but when it becomes clear I'm not going to reply, he says, "You don't need that club, Jordan. Not if you have what it gives you in real life."

The Club? This is about the Club? How the fuck?

Still, I remain quiet.

"New girl? What do you say?"

I stand up, throwing my napkin down on my unused silverware, and button my suit coat. "I think I'm leaving now."

When I get outside and look around, still confused and stunned, he's behind me, hand on my arm, pulling me into an alley. He slams me up against the brick building, places his hands around my neck, and leans in like he's gonna kiss me.

But he doesn't kiss me. His mouth finds my ear and he says, "I will pursue you relentlessly. I will not take no as an answer, Jordan. So stop fighting me and just give in."

I slap his hands away from my face, tug on my suit coat, and say, "Go home to your wife."

I end up at Chella and Smith's house down on Little Raven Street. It's one of those million-dollar townhouses just on the other side of Union Station. Planned community-type neighborhoods that attract young up-and-coming couples.

It's raining hard when I press the doorbell and peer into the long, slim window on the side of the door.

I see Smith stop what he's doing in the kitchen to look at the door, then put something down on the counter and wipe his hands on his jeans as he walks down the hallway, their husky dog, Joe, trailing him as he hops down the three stairs to the front door and opens it.

"Jordan?"

I hold out a bouquet of flowers as an offering. "Sorry I haven't been by sooner to see Chella and the baby. Is this a good time?"

"Jordan?" Chella calls from the other room.

Smith looks annoyed when I smile and push past him, but I don't care. Smith and I are only acquaintances. It's Chella I come to see.

I find her nursing her new baby in the back living area, all curled up on their overstuffed couch with her legs underneath her. She smiles big at me. "Finally!"

"I'm sorry," I say, leaning down to kiss her on the cheek. Then I point to the flowers and say, "I know I'm like two months past due, but things just really got busy."

"Yes, that game was amazing. Well done, Wells. Well done."

"Yeah." I smile. "And you played your part perfectly," I say, sitting down next to her.

"Well, whatever game you're here to rope her into now, she's not interested," Smith says. He's got his arms crossed over his chest, scowling at me as he half-sits, half-leans on the edge of the couch arm. "And she's busy. So make it quick, Wells."

Like I said, he and I… we're not really friends.

"Smith?" Chella says, looking up at him. "Can you take Daniel and put him to bed for me?" She smiles bigger. I want to glance at Smith, because I'm sure he's probably silently mouthing a litany of things like, *Get him the fuck out of here*, or *No, I'm not leaving you alone with him*. But I don't dare break her spell, so I force myself not to.

Smith grumbles something about… something, but he takes the baby and disappears upstairs, their two Yorkies and the husky following on his heels.

"So what's up?" Chella asks, fixing her nursing blouse.

I sigh, then let it all spill out as fast as I can because I know Smith is gonna come back and kick me out, and I really need a third party to give me some advice right now.

So I tell her a little bit of backstory—she already kinda knows this part and there's no point in rehashing that shit—and then move on to explain the building, and Augustine's offer, and how weird they're both being.

Two minutes later she nods her head at me, understanding.

I think.

I hope.

"I just want that club, Chella."

"You should've bought it when we were selling if you wanted it that bad." That's Smith, who is back now, leaning up against the kitchen island looking like… like a hot dad who belongs on the glossy cover of a men's magazine. It's just jeans and a t-shirt. He doesn't even have shoes on… but goddamn, Smith is the only guy I know who makes me want to be someone other than myself.

And he's absolutely going to throw me out of his house in the next five minutes, so I need to appeal to his… I dunno, something. Curiosity? Maybe he misses flying his freak flag?

I start there. "Don't you miss it?" I ask.

"No," he says.

But in that very same moment Chella says, "Kinda."

I almost laugh out loud. Because Smith gives her this look like… I can't even explain it. It's something in between shock, admiration, confusion, and desire.

I'm not kidding. I got all that from one expression.

Smith blinks. Twice. "What?"

"I'm not saying I want to fuck other people, Smith. But I miss the place. I miss the restaurant, and the bar, and…" She shrugs. "I don't want to fuck other people, but—"

She looks at me and my eyes go wide, because Smith owns a bunch of gyms now and he's built like he's on steroids—except he's not—because his job these days is basically letting at-risk teenage boys take a shot at beating the shit out of him in the boxing ring to keep them off the streets.

I put up my hands to protest—like, no. I'm not gonna join you two in a threesome—but she says, "That game with Issy… uh-huh. I'm on board with her fantasy."

Now it's my turn to blink.

Issy played a game she didn't know she was playing and most of that had nothing to do with her secret fantasy, which was being fucked in a sex club in front of other people.

I glance at Smith to gauge how he's gonna take this news, but he's just scratching his chin, like he's considering her confession.

Then he notices me noticing him and says, "Get out."

"Yes," I say. "I'm leaving." Usually I'd kiss Chella on the cheek to say goodbye, but no. "Thanks for listening, Chella."

"Thanks for stopping by!" Chella says. "And thank you for the flowers. Next time we talk I'll introduce you to the baby properly. But Jordan—" She pauses so I'll stop my retreat and look at her. "Stop running from them. That's not you. Just… just hear them out and see what it is they really want. Because they want something and whatever that is, it's some deep secret they aren't ready to share yet. That's my take on all this. It's shame, maybe. Embarrassment. Something like that. Who knows? But they're keeping it close. So you just have to wait until it comes out before you can really make a decision about this."

Then she smiles and Smith has me by the arm and he's pulling me back down the hallway towards the front door.

When we get there, he opens it up, shoves me outside, and I'm just about to turn and go down the front porch steps when he says, "Here," and thrusts a plain white envelope at me.

I look at what he's offering me, then glance up at his face. "What?"

"This," he says, shoving the envelope into my hand. "Payment."

"For what? Staying away from your wife? Get real, Smith."

"No. For killing her father." Then he smiles. "I owe you one, Wells. So if you ever actually need something—because I know you don't need money and that's what that is"—he nods to the envelope as I lift the flap and see a check written out to me. There's seven digits on that check—"I'm your guy."

Then he claps me on the back and shuts the door in my face.

I skip down the steps and walk across Little Raven Street to get in my car thinking of all the things I should've said back about that little remark. *I didn't kill him,* is the first. But then again… I sorta did.

My phone buzzes in my pocket once I'm back on Speer Boulevard heading towards the Country Club neighborhood I live in. When I get to a red light I check it.

Augustine: Before you walk away let me explain.

The light turns green, so I don't have time to fuck with a reply. But three more texts come in in quick succession.

Augustine: Don't walk away without knowing the whole story.

Augustine: You WILL want to hear this.

Augustine: I'm at your house.

Fuck.

And I'm there before I know it, pressing the button to open the gate and pulling into my driveway. Her car has to be parked on the street, but the walking gate doesn't have a lock. So she's standing under the cover of my small front porch behind a curtain of rain because it's pouring down like sheets right now.

I park, get out, and walk around to the front of the house wishing… wishing they'd just go away.

Which is ironic, because last year around this time I thought I wanted this. I thought reconnecting would be awesome.

Even though she's under the porch, she's drenched. Her long, dark hair is plastered to her wet cheeks. Water is beaded up on her upper lip and soaking her clothes.

"What the fuck, Augustine? Go home. You're gonna get sick or something."

She shakes her head and says, "No," as I unlock the door and hold it open for her.

I don't want to invite her inside but dismissing her seems out of the question.

Stop running from them. That's what Chella said. And Chella's instincts are usually right on the money. I don't really feel like I'm running, but maybe I am? And maybe they do have a secret they're keeping safe. Maybe I should just… wait them out until they're ready to spill it?

She goes inside and stands in the grand foyer, dripping on my travertine-tiled floors, hugging herself to ward off the cold.

I take my coat off, hang it up, and then say, "Well, what is it?"

"What?"

"The whole story. What is it? Because I gotta tell you, Augustine, I don't think there's anything you could tell me that would make me change my mind about this. But Chella says you guys are probably keeping a secret you're not ready to tell me yet, so…" I shrug. "If that's the case, you'd better come clean quick, because I'm about done playing."

She looks past me, into the office I'm using as my apartment. "Can we sit down at least? And can I ask you… can I have some dry clothes? I walked over here."

And even though I have a million questions about that—starting with, *Where the fuck do you live?*—I don't ask any of them. Just go into my office and start rummaging around for some sweat shorts and a t-shirt. I throw them at her and point to the office bathroom. "You can change in there."

She doesn't. She strips right in front of me, peeling off her wet clothes one layer at a time until she's standing there, naked flesh bumpy from the chill. Teeth chattering as she messes with the shorts and shirt, pulling them on and then hugging herself again.

"Do you have a blanket?" she asks.

"Welcome to my bed," I say, pointing to the couch.

And then we both kinda laugh.

It's stupid, I know this. Living the way I do. But the tension between us melts a little, and I grab the blanket, sit down, pat the cushion next to me, and wait for her to join me before covering us both up with it.

She leans into me automatically.

I let her. Automatically.

I can't deny that it all feels very familiar when we're together. Not just her and I, but Alexander as well.

We spent over two years together. That's not nothing.

"So what is it?" I ask. "This amazing story you need to tell me."

She draws in a breath. Like she needs it for courage. Then starts talking as she lets it out. "Alexander has changed a lot since you knew him."

"Has he?" I ask. "Has he really? Because it's all the same to me."

"Did you ever… did you ever…"

"Did I ever what?" I ask, getting impatient with her stammering.

"Did you ever wonder who was the top? In our relationship."

My brow creases as I think about that. "No, I guess not. It wasn't really like that. At least I didn't think it was."

"I didn't think it was either. But after you left… there was… some… maybe…"

"Goddammit, Augustine, just spit it out."

"He got dominant," she says.

"Like how?"

"Like… you know. Choking and—"

"What?"

"—face-slapping and—"

"What?"

"—and no bondage. Not that kind of dominant. But like… total throat-fucks and—"

"What?"

"—and we had a few threesomes and they were really… um, wow, like *intense* and—"

"Jesus Christ, Augustine. What are you saying? Did he hit you? Scare you?"

"No," she says quickly. "No, no, no. That's not what I'm saying. Not exactly, anyway."

I turn to face her, unwilling to accept where this might be going. "Not exactly how?"

"He's just… very… rough, Jordan."

"So he hit you?"

"No." She shaking her head. "I'm not here to complain about it. You're misunderstanding me."

"OK," I say, leaning back into the cushions to put some distance between us. "What the fuck are you trying to tell me?"

"The reason…" She sighs deeply. "He's going to kill me—not literally," she jokes, which I do not find funny. Like at all. "For telling you because he wanted to be there when we did that. Together. But I think you're about to bail on us and I don't want you to do that without hearing this first." She looks at me. Swallows hard and stares into my eyes. "Hearing why we need you."

I stare back at her. My eyes searching hers as they dart back and forth.

"He won't… engage," she finally says.

"Engage?" I ask. "What do you mean?"

"With me. That's why he won't fuck me."

"I don't understand. He's afraid of… oh, fuck. He's afraid of *losing control*?"

Augustine swallows hard again and nods her head. "Yes. He did scare me once. I… I got lost in the scene, ya know? It all became too real and… I dunno, I freaked out. And ever since then he's refused to fuck me."

I just stare at her.

"It's been almost three years, Jordan. We almost divorced over it."

"Because he hurt you?" I ask.

"No," she insists. "He didn't hurt me. He just scared me. And it was so fast, ya know? That line between fantasy and reality was so thin at that point, I just… I didn't know what to do, and I started crying and shaking and… and it was *bad*."

"Holy shit."

"Yeah. It wasn't anyone's fault, OK? We'd agreed on the scene before we played it out. I knew what was happening. And I don't know why I didn't use my safe word, but I didn't."

"Shit," I say. Because I don't know what else to say.

"And it's been hard, OK? I'm not going to lie. I love him. I really do. I do not want to divorce my husband. I love him. But he doesn't trust himself. He won't do any of the things we used to enjoy anymore. Just refuses," she says.

"So…" Jesus Christ. I'm trying to wrap my head around this and it's not easy. "So you need me to… what?"

She shrugs. A big one that lasts too long. Her shoulders hunched up near her ears, her mouth pressed together, eyes on me. "We need a third, Jordan. Or we won't survive. He wants you to make sure he stays in line. He won't ever fuck me again unless we can find a third."

"Did you… look for others?"

"Of course," she says. "We didn't just throw away our lives in LA and come here without trying everything we could think of first. Of course we tried. But he's so…" She holds up her hands, palms out, like she doesn't know what to say. "He's so strong, Jordan. The other men, they couldn't control him. Or at least he felt they couldn't. He didn't trust himself. But you. You can, Jordan. You're the only one who can."

"Wow," I say after several seconds of silence. "OK. You got me. I didn't see that coming."

"I'm begging you, OK?" She grabs onto my upper arm and leans in to me. "Begging. You. To just try. For a few weeks, that's it. And then if you want, I'll sell you the building. No matter what. If this works or doesn't. I will sell you the building. I just… I don't want to give up on him yet. I love him, Jordan. And we both still love you. We've moved past all our mistakes."

Which makes me huff out a laugh. Because it suddenly makes so much sense. "I guess you'd have to, right? Move past, I mean. Since apparently I'm the only hope you have."

"That's not why," she says. "I do forgive you. It was all… stupid and childish—"

"No," I say, cutting her off. "It wasn't. Not to Ix it wasn't. I fucked up his life pretty bad and—"

"You didn't kill his family, Jordan. It was—"

"Just stop, OK? I'm not that dumb. I don't feel responsible for a fucking car accident. But the fact that he was in jail when it happened, that his family all died that day thinking he was something he wasn't, thinking he was *me,* that *was* my fault. And look, I'm grateful that he's still in town. That he's…" I have to stop and reword my thoughts. Because we're not really friends again. "That he's considering the possibility that we might be friends again."

"I've talked to him. Several times actually since we came to Denver. He was reluctant with me. Like… he just wanted to leave me in the past. But you… not you, Jordan. And he's definitely forgiven you. Whatever it is you've been doing over the past several months with these games—he won't tell me specifics—well, it's made him pause and think hard about what we all lost back in LA. And what we could have again. How life could be better if we were all back together again."

"He's not going to play this game with us, I can tell you that right now. He's happy."

"Not the sex part. The friendship part. And it's not a game," she says, staring at me intently. "I'm not asking you for a game, Jordan. This is real. What I need from you is real. And if you decide it's not how you saw yourself, this type of relationship isn't for you, well, then fine. Alexander and I will… whatever. But I hope you'll at least take it seriously while we're trying. It's not a game. If one of us loses, we all lose. Those are the stakes. That's how it has to be."

She looks very sad tonight. Defeated. And that's not a word I'd ever use to describe Augustine before she came back into my life. So I don't bother telling her the truth. She doesn't want to hear it.

But I know how this will end. The same way it always ends when I enter a plural relationship. Broken in pieces.

"Did you even care about me?"

"Of course," I say. "Of course I did. Why the fuck do you think I went to such lengths? I mean… yes. Just yes."

"But you don't anymore?"

"It's not… just. Fuck. I've just moved on, that's all. And I don't want to look back. It was a bad time in my life. I wasn't proud of myself. I was… what I did was just shameful. You two are part of that, through no fault of your own, but you are."

"Well, thanks a lot," she says.

"I don't mean it like that. It was my shame, not yours. Not ours, either. I don't feel any shame for that."

I'm not sure that's a hundred percent true. Back then, anyway. Now, who gives a fuck? I have my friends. I have my place in the world. But back then I didn't. I was still looking for it.

"I felt a lot of things, Augustine. Too many. Too much, maybe."

"But?"

"But they're gone now."

Lies. I tell as many as they do.

They're not gone. Not completely. It's hard to put it behind me because her pull, it was strong then and it's still strong now.

She reads me. Knows me too well. I can't hide the thoughts in my head. Not from her. Because a moment later she's climbing into my lap, her face buried in my neck, her lips on my skin, nipping and kissing and biting me just the way she used to.

"Stop," I say.

"No," she whispers. "I want you." She places both palms on my face and looks me in the eyes. "I want you. Please don't send me away tonight. Let me stay. Let me put you inside me. Please."

I say nothing. Unsure what the protocol is for something like this.

Please, she silently mouths.

I take out my phone and hold it out to her. "Call and ask him," I say. Because I want to fuck her and I can't. Not unless he says yes.

"Come on," she says. "You don't need to ask permission. That's the whole point, Jordan. That you take what you want and keep him in line. Don't give him power."

"It's… cheating," I say.

"It's not cheating. You two will talk it out tomorrow. I don't know what he'll say to you, because he's unpredictable like that. He never plays along the way he's supposed to. But tomorrow night the three of us will be doing this together. Just… don't give him any power. Please," she whispers again. "Fuck me."

I'm not normally someone who runs. OK? I'm not. And I'm not normally a man who wants a woman who isn't his. That's not me. And I'm not a guy who fucks a married woman. Ever.

Unless I have permission, of course.

Augustine is tugging on my suit coat. Pulling it down my arms. I lean forward and help her take it off me. She's squirming in my lap, driving me a little crazy as I think about whether or not I actually have permission.

But then her fingers are loosening my tie. I stare up at her pretty face. Her smooth, glowing skin. She was pale when she came in out of the rain but now, charged up with the warmth of my clothes, and my blanket, and my body, she's almost flushed.

She unbuttons the shirt slowly.

And each time her fingernails brush against my bare chest I come up with a new reason to justify this behavior.

He's part of the plan.

He has to know she's here.

Hell, he was trying to fuck me earlier tonight.

It's all good…

Augustine opens my shirt and bends her back, so her head can bow down and her lips can kiss my stomach.

Holy fuck. I forgot how good she was.

My hands find a place on the top of her head, pressing her down as I raise up my hips.

She looks up at me from under her hair—knowing I'm not going to stop her—and smiles as she scoots off the couch, kneels down between my legs, and places her mouth over my hardened cock, licking it through my pants.

"You know," she says, pausing to look up at me again. She bites her lip. And damn, that alone might make me come. "If he were here he'd suck your cock too."

She whispers that last part. Like it's a secret.

"I don't think so," I say, picturing Alexander back when we used to fuck her together. "He was never really into me. He was into you *and* me. That's all."

"But you're in charge now, Jordan. You could… make him."

Imagining Alexander sucking me off with her, at the same time… OK. Yeah. I could get on board with that. But the part that really turns me on is telling him to do it.

I scoot down a little, wanting to lie back. Augustine has my pants unbuttoned and her hands reaching in for my cock.

She grabs it. Squeezes it tight. My hips rise up automatically. Urging her to give me more.

I don't want to fuck around, I just want to fuck. I want her to suck my dick for a couple minutes and then I want to bend her over the couch and take her the way Alexander wouldn't.

She obviously has other ideas. Because her tongue slowly extends from between her wet lips and flicks against the tip of my head. Teasing me. Back and forth until I close my eyes, grit my teeth, and force her head down. Force her to take me inside her mouth. All the way to the back of her throat.

Augustine is a sexual being. Has always been that way. And she takes this challenge seriously. She opens up, allows me to place her as deep as I want, muscles in her throat seizing up, gag reflex engaged… but she does not pull away.

Saliva spills down her chin and pools onto my skin where my shaft meets my balls. I close my eyes, enjoying that feeling. How it drips over my balls.

And picture Alexander doing this to me instead of her.

How far would he take me in his throat? How far would he let me push him? How far would he go before he said no?

I've always been into men. Not all men, but some. Like Bric. Like Ixion, even though he never returned those feelings. And Alexander. I never liked him, but I did like what we did in private with Augustine. And back in LA there were many nights I fell asleep masturbating to what it would feel like to have him suck my cock.

Now I'm going to get my chance.

He's here, not because he wants me. But because he wants her. And all those things he never wanted to do before could be the first way I challenge him.

I groan and say, "Stop," as my hands reach out, lift the t-shirt over her head, and grab her tits so hard, she gasps. "Take off those shorts and sit in my lap."

She smiles. And that smile is filled with approval, and submission, and promises of many more things to come.

I watch her, my fist pumping up and down my shaft, as she wiggles the shorts over her hips and lets them fall to the floor at her feet.

One knee on one side. Other knee on other side. And then her soft, wet pussy is touching my cock.

Her hands go to my shoulders. Her gaze locked on mine. She digs her fingernails into my flesh as her hips begin to move back and forth along my dick.

"I'm going to fuck you now," I say.

And then I stand up, walk her over to the window, press her back against it as she hikes her legs up to let me grab her behind the knee—and that's exactly what I do.

I fuck her standing up, her back pressed against the window. My pants fall over my hips and fall to my knees where they get stuck.

I fuck her, half undressed, soft light filtering in from the outdoor landscape lighting. Illuminating her back. Making her skin shimmer like some unearthly fantasy sex goddess.

She is moaning as I thrust forward and back. Deep, deep inside her, then almost to the point of pulling out.

She's moaning, "More, deeper, faster, harder," to the rhythm of my thrusts.

But I don't give her what she wants.

Because I don't have to.

She has put me in charge.

She should've thought about that more carefully, because I really, *really* like to be in charge.

And yeah, I'll make sure Alexander doesn't cross his line.

But right now… he's not here to make sure I don't cross mine.

I spin around, take her over to the couch, kicking off my shoes and letting my pants fall away as I walk.

Throw her down, hair falling over her face.

Grab her by the hips, flip her over.

Push her face first into the cushion, hold her there until she stops squealing.

And then I lift her hips up, slap her inner thighs to make her open her legs, and smack both hands down on her ass cheeks with a loud crack.

"Oh," she cries.

There are perfect, red handprints on her skin.

I slap her again. Same exact place.

"Oh, God," she cries, this time between clenched teeth.

Then again, even harder.

"Ow," she screams.

I grab her hair and pull it, yanking her neck back and turning her head so she has to look at me. "Is this what you want?" I ask. "You want me to be in charge of you and your husband?"

"Yes," she moans. "Yes. Please. Fuck me! Fuck me!"

It's almost not fair. For like one-eighth of a second I think that. It's almost not fair. Because he hasn't fucked her in so long, she doesn't care what I do right now.

She just wants my cock inside her. Pounding her into climax.

And besides, who cares?

Who fucking cares about fair?

I stick two fingers inside her, taking this cue directly from watching Alexander last weekend. And then I pump her hard and fast with them. In and out, back and forth across her pussy.

She squirts immediately.

And I laugh.

A loud, possibly insane laugh.

Because I have the power.

Because they gave it to me.

Because I know her body and her mind.

Because I will abuse everything about this situation.

I am, and have always been the bad guy in this relationship. We all know this.

If that's what they want, that's who they'll get.

CHAPTER SIX

"Oh, my God," she screams as she squirts. "Yes!"

You know, the usual stuff. None of it impresses me. I mean, I like fucking her. Her body is quite nice, her breasts large enough to look good in plunging-neckline shirts and dresses. They are like ripe fruit. Honeydew. Something so pretty and smooth, you can't help but touch it.

Her nipples are tight and two shades darker than her skin. Peaked up like little monuments. A testament to how much she's enjoying this.

"I want you inside me," she moans.

I'm sure she does.

"More. Again. More." She's begging me. How long has Alexander been priming her to get this kind of… sexual desperation?

And it's not like he doesn't get her off, he just doesn't give her cock.

"Does he stick things inside you?" I whisper, my fingers slower now. So she can think about this.

"What?"

"Things, Augustine. Long, hard things to make you think about the cock you're not allowed to have."

"Uh… no," she whimpers. "No. But I want more right now, Jordan. Just please. Don't play with me. Just give something freely for once."

I huff a small amount of air through my nose to simulate a laugh. "This is your game, remember? Not mine."

She exhales. Meets my gaze. Holds it for several seconds. With difficulty. Because I'm still fingering her. Still making her crazy. "You can write the rules," she says, her voice trembling. "I don't care. You can make all the rules you want. Tomorrow. Just give me what I need tonight."

I pull my fingers out and she bites her lip, whimpering. "No."

But I just smile. "I'm on board with this plan," I say. "But I'm not going to make it easy for him. Or you," I add. Because I'm feeling generous and that bit of truth is a gift. So she can prepare herself for what will happen.

She frowns.

"I might fuck you again tonight," I say, throwing her a bone. "But I want to do something else first."

"What? What do you want to do?"

I smile as I reach down, find my phone in my pants pocket, and pull up the camera. "Let's make some evidence, Augustine."

And then I laugh. Because that expression on her face is funny.

"What?"

"A little video for your husband."

"What? Why?"

"Because if I were him it would piss me off. Especially since he's the one who wanted to play the game."

She starts to turn around and face me. "We don't need—" But I yank her hair and push her face into the couch back.

"Stay right where you are," I say. "I wasn't really asking your permission, Augustine. I was telling you what comes next."

It occurs to me then... I should make them sign a contract. There's so many ways for this to get messy. And I am nothing if not a great lawyer.

But first, the video.

"Smile," I say. "We're rolling."

I do fuck her later. But only after I get a nice point-of-view video of her sucking my dick. Only after I gag her with it. Only after I come on her face. Only after I email all that beautiful footage to her husband.

And after that I send her home to deal with the consequences.

I have to admit—the whole Make My Husband Jealous game isn't one I've done before. Never played one myself. Never facilitated one for someone else. Never even thought about it, actually.

I'm calling this game... the Divorce.

Which makes me laugh.

I know, I'm a heartless asshole, but I'm not the one who started this. I was perfectly willing to walk away from them. I was more than happy to let them live their lives without me.

They started this.

My phone rings so I reach over and pluck it off the bedside table. It can only be one person.

"Yes," I say.

"Is this how you're going to play?" Alexander growls at me. "Dirty?"

I laugh again. "Did you think I wouldn't?"

"She told you then?"

"Didn't you talk to her?"

"She's with you."

"No," I say. "I sent her away about an hour ago."

"She… she never came home," he says.

I sit up in bed. "Well, where the fuck would she go?"

"I dunno." And when he says that I can picture him. Like perfectly in my mind's eye. The way he was back in LA. Younger, but really no different. He was always one of those broody assholes. Always aloof, and distant, and dark. "We're… we're not really close these days, in case you haven't noticed."

I swing my legs out of bed and put him on speaker as I find a pair of jeans and pull them on. "Well, there has to be some fucking place she'd go. A friend's house? A hotel? Does she disappear often when you two play this fucked-up game?"

"It's not like this is typical, Jordan. I don't know. She's never not come back before."

"What do you mean? What's that mean? Come back? Why does she leave?" For a second I picture him hitting her. Being violent and scaring her.

"We argue," he says. "A lot. You know we were separated."

"What kind of arguments?" I ask. "Violent ones?"

"No," he says. And I believe him. Because there's no defensiveness in that denial. No incredulous how-dare-you-accuse-me going on here. It's just kinda sad. "I called her," he says. "Before I called you. Just to see if she was coming home tonight. I think she's got her phone turned off because it went straight to voicemail."

"Hold on," I say, pressing the screen of my phone so I can put him on hold and make another call. I find her contact, press it, and yup. Sure enough, it goes straight to voicemail.

I end the call and get Alexander back. "Alexander," I say. "Where the fuck would she go?"

"I dunno… maybe a hotel?"

"What kind of hotel? Four Seasons kind of hotel? Or Motel 6 kind of hotel?"

There's a difference and it's got nothing to do with the cost of the rooms or service at the front desk. Four Seasons is an I'm-staying-put hotel. Motel 6 is an I'm-getting-the-fuck-out-of-here hotel.

"Something luxury. I guess."

I look at the clock and pinch the bridge of my nose. It's two-fifteen AM. "I have to be in court tomorrow at eight-thirty. I don't have time to go looking for your wife. Now fucking think harder. Where the hell is she? Because I won't be able to sleep if I don't know where she is."

"I'm surprised you even care."

"Don't be an asshole. Of course I care. She's not… she's not nobody to me. OK? I'm only doing this because you two fucked-up assholes wanted it. And you have something I want. It's a goddamned business deal, Alexander. That's all. And when I get what I want I'll leave you two. Disappear just like I did back in LA."

"You mean leave us to pick up the pieces."

I huff out a small laugh. But it dies pretty quick. "I said I was sorry for that. OK? And besides, I wasn't the one who started this all up again. I walked away, you two came back."

"Hold on," he says. "I think she's home." And then I hear him call out, "August!"

And from some distance away, I hear her soft voice call back. "It's me."

"OK," Alexander says. "She's here. Go back to sleep."

And then he ends the call.

There is no sleep to be had.

Not a wink.

So I get up early—like fucking four-thirty—and take a shower to wash her scent off me.

But the whole time, like from the moment he hung up on me to this moment right here, I'm thinking about all this.

Did they plan that? Was that Alexander's counter-move? Did I just take a knight and lose a bishop?

What kind of game are they really playing?

All I know is it's two against one here.

Mr. and Mrs. Alexander Bartos vs the state of Jordan Wells' mind.

Which kinda makes me laugh. Because it's stupid. But also because that's how it feels. Like I'm on trial here. Like this is more than a game to be won, but a do-or-die last-chance attempt to avoid the death penalty.

I wish I knew their motive. Why they're putting so much effort into this little scheme. How could me tearing them apart possibly save them?

And they have to know. They have to know that if they get me onboard, if I ever do really start playing for real, they're never going to win.

I mean, I'm calling it the Divorce Game for a reason. Because that's exactly what's going to happen to them.

I get dressed, skip breakfast, and go to work early, stopping by my office first, before I have to be in court.

Today isn't too difficult as far as work goes, which is good because I'm very distracted.

I just can't get the idea that they're setting me up out of my mind. Like… all this bullshit about them loving me is just that. Bullshit. And they're actually holding that grudge even tighter now than they were before. This is some elaborate plan to take me down from the inside.

That's how I'd do it. That's how I'd ruin someone's life. From the inside.

And look, both of them went from not-even-friends to instant lovers in the span of three weeks.

I'm in court until noon. I meet with three clients and have lunch afterward with my father—I texted Alexander during a break in the morning letting him know so he didn't just show up at my fucking office.

"So what are you working on?" my father asks.

We're eating lunch at his club. No, not a sex club. Just a regular private eating place, I guess. I mean, if we were down in Greenwood Village it'd be a proper country club. With a golf course and riding stables. Tennis and racquetball courts. Shit like that. But this is downtown Denver so it's basically like a… you know, one of those really nice first-class airport lounges.

They have lots of leather couches and massive chairs with nailhead details. There's a bar on one end and a buffet of snacks and non-alcoholic drinks on the other. They have a full menu, but it's not a restaurant. Not exactly.

It's just a club. A very boring one. But it's the only one I have right now.

"Nothing very interesting," I say, studying him carefully. "I got a woman facing a felony trespass charge that will probably get dropped down to a misdemeanor. One asshole who just got his sixth DUI and who totally deserves to go to jail for that, but I took it anyway because his father works for the governor and"—I hold out my hands, palms up—"what choice do I have? And then I have this other asshole. A professor at CU who got caught doing the dirty with a student and is about to lose his tenure. The usual," I say, trying not to sigh. "How about you?"

"Swamped," my dad says. But he's smiling. "Totally and utterly swamped."

"And you love it," I say.

"You know I do."

I worry about him. He had a heart attack last year. We really thought he was gonna die. Triple bypass surgery and three months of recovery later and he was back in the office. My mother protested, as did his doctors, but you know my father.

"You should slow down," I say.

"Why? So I can die bored?" He smiles at his joke.

"Take a vacation," I say. "Go somewhere nice."

"I've been everywhere nice."

"Then go somewhere shitty."

"Son, I've seen what I've needed to see. Now I just want to do what I was meant to do."

Which means work. Being a lawyer was always a calling for him. Like the priesthood. No, that's a bad example. Like… a soldier. Yeah. Like a soldier. He's part of the army of justice.

I think he's actually used that metaphor.

Law was never my calling, it was just my inheritance. He wanted me to be a lawyer so I became a lawyer. I don't hate it. I don't wish I'd chosen something else. Not really. What else would I do?

I'm just… "I hear you," I say, replying to his statement. "Sometimes I feel like that too. And I'm only thirty-one."

"You are the one who should take some time off to see things. I never spent so much time stateside when I was your age. I was always off doing things."

By things he means Peace Corps and shit like that. Volunteer things. Good works.

"In fact, by the time you were born your mother and I were tired of traveling. Which is why we didn't take you many places when you were young. I think that's why you don't have an interest in it now."

That's not why. But I don't say that. I never followed in his humanitarian footsteps because… well, I'm selfish. I grew up in the Country Club neighborhood surrounded by other Country Club brats, went to Country Club private schools, and played on Country Club sports teams.

"I saw Chella Walcott the other day," my father says.

Just hearing her name come out of his mouth kinda startles me. "She's Baldwin now," I say, just out of habit. "She got married to Smith Baldwin."

My father nods, like he knew this but can't quite get the name right. "Now that girl, she did things as a youngster. Her parents took her all over the world."

I almost laugh. Because yeah, she did do all kinds of good works as a child. And it fucked with her head so bad, she ended up in a quad relationship with Smith, Bric, and Quin at Turning Point Club trying to put it behind her.

"So sad about her father. Did they ever figure out what happened to him?"

"They found his body up in the mountains," I say. Without emotion. Which should make me pause and reflect on what kind of man I am, because I was the one who had him killed. But it doesn't. Senator Walcott was a truly evil motherfucker. Taking him down was the least I could do for Chella.

And that reminds me of the check Smith slipped me. He gave me a million dollars.

One. Million. Dollars.

I didn't cash it. I'm not going to cash it. I don't even know how to begin explaining that money to my accountant. Besides, I didn't have the senator killed because I wanted to profit from it. He just needed to die.

That thought makes me look at my own father. Who is still talking about Chella.

He doesn't need to die. I don't want him to die. He's one of the good ones. He's someone who came into this life with more than he should and used it to make a difference. He's kinda like Smith, I decide. Ironic as that is.

And I am nothing at all like either of them.

"So…" My father starts to change the subject. I wince a little, wondering what he's going to say. Maybe something about the games I'm playing. Maybe something about how distracted I've been lately. Maybe something about—

"Alexander Bartos," he says.

"What?" I wasn't ready for that.

"He comes to see you often. What's going on with him? Is he in trouble?"

"Sorta," I say, sighing. "He and his wife are..." I shrug. Not that I'd tell him the truth, but I don't even have it in me to lie right now.

"Another divorce?" My father is frowning right now.

"What?" I ask again.

"That couple you had in your office about a month back. You were doing a divorce for them?"

"Oh," I say, remembering my lie about Lawton Ayers and Oaklee Ryan. "No, those two are actually back together."

"I knew they would be," my father says, little gleam in his eye. "So... what's going on with this Bartos man?"

"Just a favor. That's all. Nothing important."

"Are you thinking of going into marital law?" he asks.

I actually laugh out loud at that. "Absolutely not. It's just a favor."

"Are they divorcing?"

"They're not sure yet. I'm just..." What the fuck am I doing? "I'm just, you know, filling him in on all his options. That's all."

"Well, I'm very happy you had time to have lunch with me today."

"Of course, Dad." I smile at him. "Alexander Bartos can fuck off. I always have time for you."

I mean that. Like there's no word strong enough to stress how much I mean that.

"I went to the doctors last week."

"Oh?" I say. And suddenly my heart is beating too fast.

"Yes... there's... a small problem."

"What kind of problem?" I ask.

"We don't know yet. I go in for more tests tomorrow."

My world is suddenly small. Sound stops. I look at him as my vision becomes like a tunnel and everything else fades to black around the edges.

When I get home after work Augustine's car is parked on the street in front of my stupid mansion. I ignore her as I wait for the gate to open and pull in the driveway. But she pulls in after me.

We get out of our cars at the same time. Staring at each other.

This morning all I was thinking about was winning their stupid game.

But tonight… all I want to do is forget.

So I say, "Wanna come inside?"

And she says, "Yes, thank you."

I wave her into the foyer. We don't even get three steps inside—we barely manage to close the front door—before we are tugging on each other's clothes.

She wants to be fucked.

I want to forget this day ever happened.

Turns out fucking is a good way to do that.

She's on her knees. I bend her over the couch. I press her back up against the window again. I fuck her on the stairs, and in the office bathroom, and then again in the bed.

I don't make her leave this time. We fall asleep holding each other. Her dreaming about… I don't know. Saving her marriage, I guess.

Me having a nightmare about what the world will look like without my father in it.

In the morning she's already gone when I wake up. And the surprising thing about that moment, the one when I realize I'm in bed alone when I didn't go to sleep that way… *isn't* that I'm alone.

It's that I slept at all.

CHAPTER SEVEN

I spend the morning trying to convince myself everything is fine. I watch my father leave for his doctor's appointment around ten-thirty, then take clients, then wait.

I'm just not sure what I'm waiting for.

My father? To come back from the doctor's?

He won't have any news. It's just tests. They don't tell you anything when you have tests.

But at noon—exactly noon—Eileen buzzes my phone. "Mr. Bartos is here to see you, Jordan."

"Send him in," I say, pressing the intercom button and then releasing it.

He knocks on the closed door, then enters, like he took a lesson from my father. He's wearing a very nice charcoal-gray suit with a silver tie. His sandy blond hair is just the right amount of messy and his jaw is unshaven.

He looks like every bit the part he's playing. Successful, handsome, deviant.

"Come on in," I say, leaning back in my chair to appear casual. But the truth is… I have no interest in this game they're playing right now.

Alexander leaves the door open, unbuttons his suit coat as he walks across my office, and takes a seat in the left-hand chair in front of my desk. He steeples his fingers under his chin, staring at me. Our eyes meet, hold there, then both of us look away at the same moment.

"What do you want?" I ask.

"Augustine didn't come home last night."

"No shit. She was at my house."

"Ah," he says, playing coy.

"You knew that," I say. Irritated. Suddenly everything about him irritates me. And not in the usual way, either. "So just stop playing."

"She wants me to invite you to dinner tonight."

"I don't think so, Alexander." Then I sigh. "I'm tired, OK? I'm just gonna go home tonight and do nothing."

"It's at our house," he adds. "She wants you to come to the house."

I don't even know where they live and the thought of fighting traffic tonight just annoys me further. Especially when I know how it's gonna end. They're gonna do something weird, I'm gonna decide I've had enough, and then I'm gonna walk out. And that's probably all going to happen before we eat, so I won't even make it to dinner. Then I'll have to stop somewhere to pick up food, or order delivery, or go hungry—and honestly, I'm just not up to it.

"My answer is still no," I say. "I'm just tired. Just tell her I'm tired."

"She wants you to come to dinner," Alexander repeats.

I close my eyes and pinch the bridge of my nose, sighing. Why can't they just go away? Why can't they just leave me alone?

"It's just so much bullshit," I say. Eyes still closed.

"What is?" Alexander asks.

"You two," I say, opening my eyes back up to look him in the eyes. "Both of you. You're more trouble than you're worth right now. I've got… I've got things on my mind."

"What things?"

"Things that are none of your goddamned business."

He leans back in the chair, places one foot on the opposite knee like he's settling in for a long conversation, and says, "She wants you to come to dinner."

"No," I say. "I'm not coming. I left this shit behind me years ago. I'm sorry I made such a mess of things when I left LA. I'm sorry for lying. I'm sorry for setting Ixion up like that. I'm sorry for hurting her, and you… and me, to be quite honest. I was young, and selfish, and stupid, and I'm not that guy anymore. You two bring out the worst in me. You two… you two make me someone else. Some guy I don't really like, Alexander. I'm done with the games, OK? I don't want to play. I don't even want your building. I don't know what I want, but I know what I don't want. And I don't want… *that*." I shake my head. "I can't deal with it right now." I didn't expect to say that about the building. And as it was coming out of my mouth I knew it was a lie. But now it's not anymore. It's not a lie. It's true. So I repeat it. "I don't want it."

He stares at me for a long moment. Like he's giving my little speech all his thoughtful consideration.

Such an actor.

I stand up, shuffling papers on my desk, pick them up and tap them on the table top to force them into a neat stack, then place them back on the desk. "I've gotta go. I have court," I lie.

I lie a lot, I realize. Pretty much all the time about everything.

He stands as I come around the desk to make my escape. But his arm extends as I try to move past him and then he's pulling me close to him. One hand slips inside my suit coat and wraps around my waist. Grips me. While the other is on my shoulder. I turn my head in his direction, startled. "What—"

And then he kisses me. Like a real kiss. His mouth is soft, and I can feel the stubble on his jaw rub against the stubble on mine. I hesitate for a moment, startled, unsure, and fully aware that my office door is wide open.

The hand that was inside my suit drops to the waist of my pants, tugs my belt for just a moment, then slips down to find my cock semi-hard.

I feel his mouth form a smile against my lips.

And then I kiss him back.

The second I do that he pulls away. Releases me and takes two steps back. "She wants you to come to dinner tonight."

And then he tugs on his suit coat, buttons it, turns around, and walks out.

I don't go to lunch and I don't have court today, so after Alexander leaves I have Eileen order me a sandwich from a place down the street, then sit in my office alone and just stare at it.

I think about his kiss. His offer. What it means. How much I want them to go away right now and just leave me alone.

But I also think about how much fun we had back in LA. Before I got jealous, and weird, and fucked it all up.

Are they here to get even? Or are they really here to start something new?

I'm having a hard time seeing things clearly. It surprises me because I'm so detached when I deal with people who play the game. But then again, I'm not surprised at all because this isn't my game.

I think that's the problem.

I'm not running any of this. I don't have Darrel and Finn running interference. They're not keeping tabs on shit, making sure it goes off without a hitch. I'm personally involved with the outcome.

That is definitely my problem.

At three o'clock my father returns to the office. He's smiling and his gregarious laughter fills the reception area. I can hear it all the way back in my office.

I track his voice as he makes his way down the hall towards me. Imagine him stopping to place a hand on someone's shoulder as he answers questions people ask him.

Then the knock. He enters, smiling.

"How did it go?" I ask.

"Fine," he says. "Just fine. Don't worry. I'm not worried."

"Well… what's the issue?" I ask. "Like what do they think is wrong?" He never told me last night.

My father shakes his head, still smiling. "Let's talk about that when we have to. *If* we have to. There's no point in getting upset over something that's not happening."

"Dad—"

"No," he says, putting up a hand to stop me. "I'm fine, Jordan. Just… we'll see what the tests say."

At four o'clock my phone buzzes a text. I've been sitting in my office staring at my closed door for the past hour, wondering what's wrong with my father. He's been in a good mood since he came back. I can hear him right now. Laughing down the hallway in the conference room. There's a deposition, but it hasn't started yet, so he's just chatting with opposing counsel.

I feel a little better that he's in good spirits, but not much.

I glance down at my phone screen to log the incoming text. It's an address. Augustine and Alexander's address, I can only presume.

Then… *Dinner is at 6* pops up underneath the address and it's confirmed.

I don't answer and there are no more texts.

I just sit at my desk and stare at my door.

But at five-thirty Eileen buzzes my desk phone. "Jordan? I'm leaving. Do you need anything?"

Eileen is a nice woman and a competent assistant. About thirty-five, I guess. I never asked her. Short dark hair that hangs alongside her heart-shaped face and ends at her shoulders. Curvy, pretty, and smart.

I wonder what she thinks about me? She has to know I'm running these games. I mean it's not really a secret. Plenty of people know. Enough that I get regular inquiries. And my father knows. I told him. He said just keep it legal and I have.

Mostly.

But the illegal parts are only there to keep people safe.

I press the speaker button on the phone and say, "No, I'm good, Eileen. Thanks. See you tomorrow."

She sighs on the other end. "Is everything OK?"

"Yup," I lie. Because really? What am I going to say to my assistant? We're not that kind of co-workers, ya know? Some people have an assistant as their right-hand man. Or woman. But Eileen isn't that kind of assistant. Darrel is that kind of assistant. And Darrel and Finn are off doing other things right now. Besides, none of what's happening to me right now is the kind of thing you discuss with an assistant like Darrel either. "I'm fine, really," I say. "See you tomorrow."

"OK. Have a good night."

"You too." And then I press the speaker button again.

What would a good night look like for me?

The question pops into my mind unexpectedly.

When was the last time I had a good night?

Jesus, probably back when the Club was still open. Since then I've been biding my time with these games, my friendship with Chella, and my legal career.

I don't even remember the last time I was on a date. Like a real date. Not meeting a game client, or law client, or a business associate.

Which makes me pick up my phone and open the message Augustine sent. The address is linked to my map app, so I press it, telling myself I'm just curious to see where they live.

Hmmm. Nice area. Right on Cheeseman Park. In fact, it's so close to my house I can walk there in a matter of minutes if I cut through the Botanic Gardens.

I decide to go home.

When I get to my house it's ten minutes to six.

Ten minutes and I can forget all about this invitation.

Ten minutes and I can….

What? What will I do in ten minutes? Sit here and drink some Scotch? Sit here and order food? Sit here and think about my father?

What will I do in ten minutes?

Eight minutes later I'm standing in front of their building looking up. It's a modern fifteen-story structure that looks like Frank Lloyd Wright's version of a high-rise, if he'd made the Price Tower look like Falling Water instead of Price Tower.

In a word, nice.

I go inside, get in the elevator, take it up to the top floor, and exit into a small hallway with only one set of massive double doors.

At exactly six o'clock I press the doorbell. It chimes the deep, classic half-note *ding-dong* and sounds like church bells.

I hear footsteps approach and the door opens to reveal Alexander holding a snifter and the strong scent of a well-made cognac fills the air. He smiles at me. It's a small smile, perhaps even a disappointed smile. Like he didn't figure I'd show up. "Come in," he says, opening the door wide.

I step in and look around. The ceilings are high, but not very high. This building is old. Probably built in the Thirties. Like maybe the designer was a contemporary of Wright and this was his stamp on the world of modern architecture at the time.

The ceilings are coffered, much like the ballroom ceilings in my own house, and the floors are a rich, dark hardwood that looks original. The view of the city is spectacular. Seen through an entire wall of windows, the Denver skyline is already lit up, a silhouette against the setting sun that hangs just over the top of the mountains.

"This is lovely," I say, just as I notice Augustine over in the kitchen. Someone obviously renovated this apartment because it's an open-concept layout. She's wearing a white dress and a light blue apron. She has yellow oven mitts on her hands and she's holding a baking dish. "And you look lovely as well."

I don't know why I say that except that it's true. She looks… softer somehow. I've never seen her in domestic mode. I only remember the wild girl in cut-offs and tank tops.

She is someone else now. Someone I don't know.

But I guess that's true for anyone you lose contact with and reconnect with later.

Now I smell the food and my stomach grumbles. I never did eat that sandwich at lunch.

"Thank you," she says, smiling at me.

"Want to take off your coat?" Alexander asks me. His hands are already on my shoulders, ready to help. I let him slip the suit coat down my arms and then he walks over to a closet near the front door and hangs it up.

"I hope you're hungry. I made way too much. But I'm glad you came." She pauses to laugh. "Because I made way too much."

"I am, actually." It's all I can think of to say. I don't know them anymore. This is clear. When we were last together it was something altogether different. They've been living as a couple for almost eight years now. Married, separated, back together. A lifetime apart is what this feels like.

"Sit down," Alexander says, pointing to the dining room table. It's small, which is surprising. And round. Seats maybe… four? But there's only three chairs there now. I look around the room, trying to find the missing one. No one buys three chairs. But it's… missing. If they have a fourth chair, it's hidden and out of view.

"Do you want a drink?" Alexander asks.

"Sure. What you're having is fine." I say it as I watch Augustine place a rack of lamb onto a large white platter, take off her oven mitts, and then look up to find me staring. She smiles, reaching behind her back to untie her apron. She hangs it up on a hook inside the pantry and then picks up the platter and walks towards me. "Sit," she says. Because I'm still standing.

I do. Taking one of the chairs just as Alexander returns with my snifter of cognac and she places the platter in the center of the table. She smiles at me one more time and then Alexander holds her chair out and pushes it in for her before taking his seat.

She's on my left, he's on my right.

They have thoroughly planned this evening, I decide.

"What did you do today?" Alexander asks.

I look over at him, thinking he's talking to me, but he isn't. He's asking his wife.

"I took meetings," she says quietly. "With contractors."

"Contractors?" I ask. "For what?"

"The building," she says.

I look over at Alexander, who just shrugs. "I don't know either. She's been playing coy with me about the whole thing."

"My building?" I ask.

She meets my gaze and says, "It's not your building."

"But you're selling it to me. I'm here, playing your game, so in three weeks you're selling it to me. That's what you said."

"These arrangements were already in place. It's just… motions, Jordan. Going through motions."

"What arrangements? What motions? You're not tearing shit down in there, are you? I mean, for fuck's sake, Augustine—"

"Don't bother," Alexander says, interrupting me. "She's trying to rile you up."

Augustine makes a face at him then turns to me. "I'll keep my word. And nothing's been changed yet. I'm just making plans."

"What plans?" I ask.

"If everything goes the way it's supposed to then you won't need to worry. So just… eat. I made a lot of lamb and it's never good the next day."

She nods to Alexander and he carves the meat, dishing a portion out to each of us.

I'm suddenly not hungry. I'm suddenly ready to go home and order pizza. I'm suddenly filled with regret for even coming over here tonight.

"We had a nice kiss today," Alexander says, bringing me out of my thoughts.

I look at him, but he's looking at her.

"How nice?" Augustine asks him. They're acting like I'm not even here.

"Full mouth," he says, taking a bite of lamb. Then he pauses to chew. Slowly. And swallows. "I made him hard."

Augustine beams a smile at me. "Well… we're making progress. Want me to tell you what we did last night?"

Alexander nods his head. "Please."

I don't say another word through dinner. She describes our sex in explicit detail. Like we were recording it and then she took that recording home, watched it over and over on repeat, and wrote down and memorized everything she was going to say tonight.

"You're making me hard," Alexander says, standing up so we can see his proof. "Feel me," he says, walking towards her and taking her hand. He places it over his cock and she squeezes him through his pants.

I can't stop watching.

He grabs her hair. Hard. Rough. Augustine lets out a small yelp and I am immediately on my feet.

The deal we have—the one Augustine offered—is back, front and center, in my mind.

Alexander glances over at me. Aware that my reaction is one of challenge. "What?" he growls. "What will you do?"

I tilt my head at him, unsure if this is an act or if it's real. I don't allow myself to look to Augustine for clarification. That just feeds his power. "You know damn well what I'll do."

"Pretend I'm obtuse, Jordan. And spell it out."

"Keep you under control. Keep you from losing control."

He yanks Augustine's hair, jerking her head so she's looking up at him. "Do you trust him?"

I'm thrown for a moment. Because she doesn't look scared. "Yes," is all she says. And she says it in a tone that lets me know this is just business. A contractual negotiation.

"You must be sure," Alexander whispers. "Absolutely sure."

"I am," she says, placing her hand over his, which is still gripping her hair so tight, it's pulling on her scalp.

What the hell am I witnessing?

"I'm sure," Augustine repeats, staring up into Alexander's eyes. "Please. It's the only option we have left."

I squint my eyes, trying to fit those words into what I know of their relationship.

This is what I come up with:

One. They love each other. Perhaps they're even soulmates. Although if you had asked me that before this moment, I'd have laughed. But maybe I'm wrong. Because this is a lot of trouble to go through in order to save a dying marriage. Most people just assume failure is inevitable. That this was never a soulmates connection. Thus, they get a divorce. But these two are convinced they can work things out. Alexander truly is overly aggressive during sex and I truly am the only one who can control him to Augustine's satisfaction.

Two. They've separated before. Got back together. Then upended their lives in LA and moved here. For me. I'm still discovering the details behind that, but my assumption is that they equate their happiness with the time in LA when the four of us—me, Ix, and the two of them—were together. And since Ix bailed out first and has since found someone he loves and cares about, I'm the only missing piece in the puzzle that is their collective unhappiness. If they can get me, they get that love back.

Or three. Which is the big one. They're playing me. They never forgave me for what I did back in LA and they want to hurt me the way I hurt them. Perhaps they even blame me for their crumbling relationship. Perhaps they spent weeks, or months, even years of sleepless nights and endless fights over what happened. And how I just… left and moved on. Left them to pick up the pieces and put themselves all back together.

Alexander pulls Augustine right out of her chair and I take two steps towards them before I get myself under control and stop in my tracks. She's on her knees in front of him now. Looking up into his eyes like he is her fucking master.

He slaps her.

Her head doesn't move.

Was the slap just playful?

I don't think so. It was loud and there's already a red mark on her cheek. She just knows how to control herself. Her eyes never leave his.

He slaps her again—the other cheek this time.

"Stop it!" I say, crossing the distance between us. "What the fuck, Alexander?"

He looks at me and smiles. Lets go of her hair, tugs on his jacket like he's pulling himself together, and walks around the table to take his seat again.

"Get up, August," I say. She reaches for me and I help her to her feet. Her face is red, both cheeks. I pull out her chair and she sits, allowing me to push her back in. The same way Alexander did before this little display of dominance upended our roles.

I walk back to my chair and sit. Let out a long breath of air and look Alexander dead in the eyes. "This is who you are?"

He shrugs and breaks off a small piece of the roll on his plate. I glance at Augustine, who is watching him, not me, and then I look back at Alexander to find him spreading butter on the bite-sized piece of bread. He puts it in his mouth and chews, watching me thoughtfully, the anger—or whatever you call that emotion inside him he just showed us—gone.

"If you can't handle it, we'll understand," Alexander says.

Once again, I find myself looking to Augustine for... something. Clarification or, I dunno, *something*. "Do you like this?" I ask her.

She nods. Then clears her throat. "I love it, Jordan. And he won't do it anymore."

"Why?" I ask, sensing there's more to that. "Why did he stop?" She just shakes her head so I look to him. "Did you hurt her? Crossed a line and then promised never to do it again?"

He shrugs. "You're perceptive," he says. "Which, I suppose, is why she trusts you."

"How bad did you hurt her?" I ask. I feel hot all of a sudden. Anger coursing through my body. "Break her arm? Give her a black eye? Rape her?"

"Come on," Alexander says. "I love her. I wouldn't do any of that."

"Then what did you do?"

"Jordan," Augustine says. "Let's talk about that later. Let's just—"

I stand up, pounding the table with both hands. Augustine startles, jumping with the silverware. "Tell me," I growl. "Or I'll walk out right now. I won't participate in bullshit like this. I won't become *you*, Alexander."

"That's precisely the point," Augustine says. Too loud. Not a yell or shout, but too loud. "You're not him. You'll never be him," she snaps.

And for some reason I take that as an insult. That he is somehow better than me. This asshole who likes to hit her to get off is better than me.

And she allows it. She wants it. He stopped and she dragged him here. Made him leave LA and come to Denver to find me. So they can continue this… this sick version of love they've cultivated since I left.

"Look," Alexander says. "I can't help what I like. I'm sorry I ever started doing it with her. Because—"

"Because I love it," Augustine says. "It's fantasy. It's pretend, Jordan. You of all people, the fucking game master himself, should be able to see this for what it is. A game."

"A lifestyle," I correct her. "This isn't a game. This is a top-bottom *lifestyle*."

"Not really," Alexander says, then takes a sip of wine. He swallows, puts his glass down, and then continues. "Because I don't want her to submit to me. I want her to fight me."

My brain is on fire, doing an internal search for a memory of any such game. I cannot recall ever hearing about this. "Who gets to win?" I ask. Because it matters. And I need to make sense of this.

"We both win," Augustine says. "When the game is over and we're satisfied and happy."

"So… so you don't want to be tied down and… you know. Kinda forced?"

"No," Augustine says.

"And you don't want to force her?"

"God, no. It's not a rape fantasy."

"But you want her to fight you?"

"Yes. But she won't fight back," Alexander says.

"If I fight back, he stops," Augustine says.

"Because I lose control," he clarifies. "And I don't want to lose control."

"OK." I put up a hand. "Hold on here. You want her to fight you?" I look at Alexander and he nods. "You refuse to fight back." I point to Augustine.

"Because he'll stop," she says again. "I will fight back," she says, looking at Alexander. "But only if we keep going and see it through to the end."

I think about this as we all sit in silence. Then I say, "I have to admit, you guys, I've never heard of this one. I… I don't think it has a name. I'm gonna have to get some advice first. I can't—"

"No," Augustine says. This time it's her pounding her fists on the table, making the silverware jump. "No. Tonight."

"Tonight? No. Fuck that. I… I… I don't even know what this *is*."

"Well," Alexander says, placing his napkin on his plate. "We can show you."

They get up at the same time. Eyes locked. And they nod.

And once again I get that feeling about them. That they are truly connected. That they know each other so well.

He walks over to her and says, "You invited this asshole into our house?" Before she can answer he slaps her across the face again.

This time Augustine is instantly breathing heavy. Like that excites her. Which is normal, I've seen that before.

But then… but then her arm is in motion, her hand connects with his face, and her slap is much louder than his.

He grabs her wrists and I'm on my feet. My heart pounding too, my head spinning at what I'm about to witness. He pushes her backwards until she bumps into the back of the couch. He pushes her again, hard, and she falls backwards, legs in the air. Alexander has his hands up inside her dress, pulling on her panties. She either lets him get them off, or it's possible he's just that quick, I'm not sure. But as soon as her panties go flying over his shoulder, she connects a flat-footed kick to his chest.

I know that hurts. I can feel it from here.

He grabs her legs, spreading them open. Augustine is still upended. Head and shoulders on the couch cushions, knees bent over the back of the couch, Alexander's hands on her ankles.

She begins to kick and grunt, but he reaches down and grabs her long hair with both hands, pulling her back up so she's now sitting on the back of the couch, her eyes level with his chest.

Her fingers go to his shirt, ripping it open. Buttons go flying and Alexander tries to back away, but she holds tight, refusing to let him.

I'm… I dunno the word for it. Stunned? Mesmerized?

"That's enough," he says. "That's enough."

"No," Augustine begs. She's on her feet, still holding the two flapping ends of his open shirt. Leaning up on her tiptoes, trying to kiss him.

He shakes his head, pries her hands off him, and then backs away, breathing heavy and hard as he turns to me. "There," he says. "That should give you an idea."

"Don't stop!" Augustine says. "Come on! He's here. He's—"

"He's got no fucking clue, August!" Alexander practically shouts. It's loud enough to stop her begging.

She lets go of his shirt and sits down on the back of her couch, twirling her body so she can flop down onto the cushions.

"Uh…" I say.

"Yeah," Alexander says, taking off his suit coat and throwing it over a dining room chair. He takes off his shirt too. And I get a little stuck on the perfectly sculpted physique of his chest.

"Ahh," I try again. "I think you two are fucking crazy."

"Fuck you," Augustine spits. But she's not looking at me. She's truly pissed off this… whatever it was just ended.

Alexander looks at me, then shrugs. Like he's with me, but… a girl wants what she wants. And, well, what can you do?

Get another crazy player is their answer, I guess. "Look, you guys. I don't think—"

"Then get out," Augustine snarls.

But when I look at Alexander he gives me a little shake of his head. Like… maybe this is all part of the game?

I suddenly understand how Issy Grey felt when I set her up in a game she didn't ask to play. I might need a poster slogan to help me make sense of this.

At the very least, I need to talk to Lucinda. And Chella. Because… oh, yeah. This is one for the books.

And then he… he mouths something. "What?" I ask.

He rolls his eyes at me. Then mouths it again. Slower. Exaggerated. *Fuck her.*

Fuck her… like she can fuck off? Or he's telling me to fuck his wife?

"I need to go."

"Jordan!" Augustine says, scrambling to her knees and peeking her head over the couch. "No. Stay. Come on.

You know this interests you. You know you and I have something good. And you and Alexander—"

I shake my head. "No… I don't think—"

But then… somehow… Alexander has crossed the room and he's right up next to me. His bare chest pressing against mine as he leans in, grabs my face, and kisses me.

I'm so surprised I can't even decide what I should do about this. Like… pull away? Or kiss him back? And then Augustine is sliding under Alexander's arm, inserting herself between us.

"Don't leave now," she says, her hands on Alexander's, which are still holding my face. She leans up on her tiptoes and begins kissing us. Both of us, as he kisses me and…

Jesus. I should walk. I've done so well so far. Keeping my distance from this train wreck of a relationship.

But her hand is on my cock and… and when I break away, out of the kiss, and look down, her hand is on his cock too.

And isn't this what I've wanted? Maybe not them, but this?

I don't have time to think it through.

Augustine crouches down, her legs spread open, her fingers deftly unbuttoning and unzipping my pants. And then she's got both our cocks fisted in her palms. Stroking us. Up and down and squeezing tight.

Alexander grabs her hair, pulling it hard. But when I look at him, his eyes are closed. And I know… God, I just fucking know… he's not paying attention anymore. Not like he was during their little demonstration.

And it has become my job to keep him in check.

The moment Augustine's mouth wraps around the head of his cock, he pushes her towards him. His hips rocking forward, making her take him deep. She gags and tries to pull back, but he holds her there. She lets go of my dick, reaches up for his forearm, and claws her fingernails down his skin.

Alexander hisses and pulls back, which allows Augustine to pivot and concentrate on me.

Oh, God. Her mouth on my tip feels excruciatingly good. And when she opens wide and puts me inside her… the warm and the wet… and the sucking…

And then Alexander is there, kneeling down behind her, his hand in her hair again, pushing her into me now.

Making her take me.

Making her gag on me.

And for a split second I don't see what he's doing. I don't realize what he's doing. I am too fully encapsulated in lust and desire to realize he's dragging me over to his side. Distracting me from my job by letting his wife pleasure me.

"Stop," I say, my voice hoarse.

But when I look at him he just smiles. Shakes his head a little. And then he kisses me.

I forget about August. Just… I don't know. Just let her drift away. Her mouth, my cock deep in her throat. The warm saliva pooling up against my shaft as Alexander reaches underneath my balls and cups them in his hand.

Holy fucking—

And then he punches me.

Right in the fucking mouth.

I snap.

Out of the lust. Out of the passion. Out of the desire.

And I back away, my cock slipping from Augustine's mouth as I swing and hit him back.

He ducks and rushes me, barreling into my chest until I reel backwards, slamming into a wall, just barely able to stop myself from falling.

They approach me. Slowly, as a team. Like two lions looking for a kill.

"What the fuck?" I ask. But when he's within reach, I swing again, and this time… this time that motherfucker goes down.

I climb on top of him, my cock swinging, my pants around my knees, and then his hand finds my dick, and Augustine is crouching, her pussy right over his face.

And I'm ashamed to admit this, even just to myself… but I swear to God this is hot. I'm turned on. Like rock-hard cock.

I go down on him. My mouth taking him, pressing forward the way he just showed me he likes it. Augustine is bending over a little, her ass right in front of me, his fingers probing between her legs, stroking her as she moves back and forth, fucking his face.

I pull her backward, roughly—too roughly and I'll have to think about that later, because there's no room for that now—making her squeal. I scoot her ass down until she's right over Alexander's dick and after that, she doesn't need any more hints.

She sits down on his cock, her back arched, practically begging me to pull her hair.

So I do. And when I pull too hard, she twists around, reaching back to slap my face. I swat her hand away and push her forward until she falls onto Alexander's chest.

I lean down, swipe my tongue around the rim of her ass, then spit and massage it in with my fingertips. I scoot up, Alexander's leg between mine, my balls dragging across his thighs, and push my cock inside her.

"Oh," she moans. "Oh, oh, oh...."

We are sweaty. Hot and slick. Alexander stops to let me find my way past his huge cock already inside her, and then we both begin. Slowly. Just small pushes and pulls. Barely moving.

Augustine is making noises I've never heard before. Not even when we used to do this all those years ago. I grab her hair, pull her up off his chest, forcing her to arch her back, and then wrap my other hand around her throat so I can hold her in place so I can kiss her and fuck her at the same time.

She comes.

There's no way she can't.

This is what she wants. What she's been missing.

This is why I'm necessary.

CHAPTER EIGHT

I didn't stay the night. I probably should've. Might've even enjoyed it, but staying the night is a big step forward and I'm not sure I want to move forward.

This completes them, fine. But what's it do for me? Aside from make my life more complicated?

I mean look, these two people are married. They don't want to get a divorce. They're so committed to each other they have decided adding a third is the only way to save what they have.

That's their goal.

Augustine has already tried to call me several times this morning and I've let them all go to voicemail. And I'm not at home or work, so she can't pop up and find me. At least not yet.

I just need some space to try to figure out if I want to participate. I need to think. I need…

My phone buzzes in my pocket, interrupting my thoughts. It's probably them, so when I take out my phone and check the screen, I'm pleasantly surprised to see Ixion's name come up.

"Ix," I say. "What's up?"

"Hey, you free right now? Or you busy?"

"Why?"

"Because I'm asking."

Fucking Ixion. "Sure. What do ya need?"

"Meet me at the Mile High Cafe in half an hour." And then the call ends with three quick beeps.

Hmmm. What's this about?

I'm sitting in a booth on the second floor of the Barrister Club. I'm not a paying member, but I'm on my father's list of permanent guests. And it's a great place to hide when you don't want to be disturbed. Plus, it's right across the street from the courthouse, so it's the perfect place to go between court cases and, as a bonus, the Mile High Cafe is like a five-minute walk from here.

Which gives me plenty of time to sit and stew on this impromptu phone call from Ixion. Lots of time to wonder what he's up to. Did Augustine call him? Tell him what we did last night? Is he going to warn me? Or scold me? Or tell me to back away?

I have no clue. But I can picture him doing all three, so…

When I get to the cafe Ixion already has a table near the back. So I point to him when the hostess asks me for my name. This place is crazy busy at lunch and there is almost always a wait if you're not just picking up an order.

I weave my way through the tables and take the seat across from him, thankful for the ceiling fan directly above us, because today is just a little bit too warm.

Ixion looks good. More like himself than I've seen him in almost a decade. He played a game a few months ago. Well, that's not technically true. I hired him to do surveillance on a woman named Evangeline Rolaine. A crazy violin child prodigy who couldn't perform on stage anymore because the thought of being watched terrified her. Her therapist, Lucinda Chatwell, set this game up, so it was more like treatment than a game.

Until Ixion fucked it all up, that is.

But hey, he fixed her. And they're still together so I count that as a win.

"What's up?" I say.

"Question for you," Ixion says.

"A question? Why didn't you just ask me on the phone?"

"Because I haven't seen you in a couple weeks and I wanted to check in."

"You're worried about me?" I ask, unable to hide my smile or the chuckle that comes out with it.

"A little bit," he says, holding his thumb and forefinger about a centimeter apart. "But first… you still have access to that house?"

"Which one? The mansion next to the gardens?"

"Yeah, the one we played our game in."

"Yeah, I'm kinda… living there at the moment."

"Oh," he says, considering this. Ixion is a fuck-hot dude. I'm kinda into dudes. Not all the way into dudes, but I appreciate the addition of another guy in a relationship. Which is why Augustine and Alexander came to me, right?

Well, anyway. Ixion is hot. He's got a nice build. One of those tough guys who wears jeans and t-shirts and rides a motorcycle. But the guy is fucking loaded. His family was killed in a car crash years ago, right after all that shit went down in LA, so he inherited everything. I don't even know how much money this guy actually has because he never talks about it. Never spends it either. At least not on himself. And it occurs to me… "Why?" I ask. "You wanna buy it?"

Ixion chews his lip like he's not sure. And then he says, "Maybe. I'm not sure. Evangeline is sorta fixated on it."

"Oh," I say, leaning back in my chair. "Fixated how?"

"Like… she can't stop talking about that family, ya know? All those photographs and stuff. She keeps bugging me to ask you who they are."

"I dunno." I shrug. "I bought the house on foreclosure last year. These old historic mansions almost never come up for sale so I snatched it up because… fuck, I have no idea why I bought that stupid house. None. Just… an impulse buy, I guess."

Ixion laughs. "A seven-million-dollar impulse?"

"I didn't want anyone else to have it."

He laughs louder. Because spending seven million dollars just to get something no one else has is so… *me.*

"But if you're interested in buying it, I'm definitely selling. It was a dumb idea. And I'm house-poor now and I hate it."

"Well, I don't know, man. It might be too big, ya know?"

"Tell me about it. I live in the fucking office. And I sold all the furniture so the whole place is empty."

"You sold everything?" Ix asks.

"Yeah."

"What about the photos?"

"I boxed them up and sent them over to Lawton's office. What he did with them, I have no clue. Why?"

Ixion chews his cheek for a second, thinking. "Evangeline is just obsessed. Wants to know who they are. You don't know anything?"

"No. The bank owned the house when I bought it. Their name wasn't on any of the papers."

"Huh. Well, I guess I'll have to look into it."

"Why's she want to know this stuff?" I ask.

"Well," Ixion says, then stops, like he's choosing his words carefully. "She was slightly obsessed with the family, ya know? The whole fantasy that place kinda encapsulates. I mean the house is goddamned gorgeous. And the gardens, in the backyard and next door. It's just very… perfect. She's fixated on the reason why that family left everything behind. Like, at first she thought it was like a summer home. Like maybe they lived somewhere else in the winters. But then she found out you actually owned the house, which blew that theory out of the water. So every day she's got some crazy made-up story about who these people are and where they went."

"Wow," I say, unsure what to think about all that. "She's definitely got one of those obsessive personalities, doesn't she?"

Ixion smiles, like this is just one of those quirks he loves about her. "Just a little bit. But I have another question for you. Since we're here."

"Shoot," I say, kinda loving this interaction with Ixion. It feels like maybe we turned a corner. That the past is the past and now we're… I dunno. We've forged a new, different kind of relationship.

"What the fuck are you doing with Augustine?"

"Shit, man." I sigh, shaking my head. "I don't know. She's all up in my face. Wants me to help her and Alexander…" I shrug. Because I don't really know how to explain this.

"Wants you to help them do what?"

"Like… fix their marriage? I swear, Ixion, I'm not playing here, but I feel very much like I'm playing a game. They have turned into a couple of very fucked-up people."

"And a part of you wonders if you're to blame?" Ix asks.

And the funny thing is… I don't think he meant that to be mean. I seriously think he just said it because he really thinks that's what's on my mind. "No." I huff. "Look, OK. So I lied a little back in LA. So I set you and her up just to piss off Alexander and break them apart. I get it. I was a dick. I've apologized. I walked away, left them alone, started over, tried to make good, changed my ways, blah, blah, blah. And they got married, and moved on, and separated, and got back together. Whatever. It's their life. Whatever this is they're into now has nothing to do with me."

"Wow," Ixion says, leaning back in his chair. "You're a little bit defensive, dude."

I lean in, my elbows on the table, and look him straight in the eyes. "They are a couple of fucked-up people, OK? And yeah, OK, so are we. Fine. We're all a little fucked up. But the shit they want me to do with them, Ixion. It's fuckin' weird."

"Weird how?" he asks, leaning forward again.

I'm not sure I should even try to explain it. At least to him. I should call Lucinda and get her opinion. She's the therapist who set up Evangeline's "treatment" and the whole reason why Ixion and Evangeline are together.

"Just tell me," he says. "I've already seen the weird and the ugly with you guys."

"Don't classify me with them. I mean, OK, I've got my weird and ugly side too. But don't classify me with them."

"Shit, must be serious."

I sigh, then ease forward again so now we're both leaning forward on the table. "Have you ever heard of… people… or like… a fetish where people…"

"Just fucking spit it out," Ix says.

"Where people get off on fighting each other?"

His head does that taken-aback thing and he frowns. "Fight? Like… argue?"

"No," I say. "Not like argue. Like slapping and shit?" And then he's about to say something and I already know what he's going to say, so I put up a hand to stop him. "No, not like a dominant-submissive thing, either. Because that's not the dynamic. There's no top or bottom. It's like equal top and bottom at all times."

"Like… they get off on hitting each other?" He's squinting his eyes.

I nod. "Yeah. She wants him to slap her, but he wants her to hit him back. And he refuses to engage anymore because… I dunno, he lost control once and so never again. So he stopped fucking her, I guess. Only gets her off other ways. And now they want me to join them so I can control Alexander while they play this fucking fight game with each other."

"Wow," Ix says, leaning back in his chair.

"Right?"

He makes this little whistle noise. "Yeah, that's weird."

"I think so too. But I'm gonna ask Lucinda about it. Because, get this. Fucking Augustine owns the old Turning Point Club building and I want to buy it and reopen the club, but she won't sell it to me unless I give this whole sexual moderator thing a try for three weeks."

"Hmmm," Ix says.

I sigh. But I feel a lot better telling this shit to Ix. Feels good, actually. To talk to him like a friend again and not have all the animosity between us.

"What happened to them?" Ixion asks.

"I dunno," I say. "But they make me feel responsible."

"That's bullshit. You walked away eight years ago. What they did with all that time between then and now is all on them. I mean, look, I had a pretty rough several years too. But it wasn't you who did that to me."

It's the first time he's ever hinted that he might be able to forgive me. So I stay quiet and let him talk.

"I mean… yeah. I did a lot of stupid shit and I was sad, but my sadness had nothing to do with you. And even though it didn't *feel* like I moved on, I did move on, Jordan. Maybe what I was doing wasn't like… a proper future or anything. But it was honest. Ya know?"

"I get it," I say. "And I'm so fucking sorry, man. I really—"

"You had nothing to do with the death of my family," he says, interrupting me.

Even though I've been waiting years for this confession from him, hearing it now… it fucking hurts.

"You didn't kill them. It was a stupid car accident. And if it's anyone's fault, it was that person who hit them."

"But they died thinking you were some really fucked-up creep and that part was all my fault. You took the fucking blame for me, Ixion. And I never deserved your protection like that. I never earned it."

He does a one-shoulder shrug. "It's in the past, man. Where it belongs. So just leave it there. I'm fine. I'm actually pretty fucking happy these days. And if you hadn't flown up to Wyoming and pulled my ass out of jail that day and told me to get my shit together because I was *needed*, I'd still be a worthless piece of shit. That job you gave me watching Evangeline was the very best-case scenario as far as the whole where-is-Ixion's-life-going scenario is concerned."

He reaches across the table, grabs my hair and pulls me close to him.

I am too startled—too afraid—to breathe.

He bumps his forehead to mine, then retreats. "It could've gone a million ways, ya know?"

What does that mean? I wonder. Like he'd have been into a threesome with me and Augustine if they didn't start that professional relationship together with the production company? Or… if Alexander wasn't in the picture? If it was just the three of us, and not the four of us? Or—

"Don't waste your time, Jordan," Ix says. "It doesn't matter what it could've been. This is just what it is now. And it's good, ya know? It's just fine."

I reach over and grip his shoulder. "I will never forget what you did for me, Ixion."

"I'm calling it even." And then he smiles, stands up, and says, "Don't let them drag you into the past, Jordan. If you want to play their little game then reinvent it. Play on your own terms. Don't let them ruin what you've got going. Because you built something good here, brother. I'm proud of you."

And with that, the conversation is over.

Because he gets up and walks out.

Play the game if I want. But play it on my own terms.

In other words, be the goddamned game master.

My next stop is Lucinda. She's not your typical psychiatrist at all. For one thing, she's got this little side business going called What Are You Afraid Of? She fixes people's fears and most of her games—no, they're not games, I decide—most of her *patients* are cured with sex therapy. Not all of them, but Lucinda maintains that almost all our hang-ups go back to some kind of sexual dysfunction.

I was sort of a silent partner in that little business with her. Just a front man. She had these business cards printed up. They were the size and thickness of a drink coaster you'd find in Oaklee Ryan's Bronco Brews bar, with fancy engraved lettering, and all they said on the front was *What Are You Afraid Of?* On the back she had her contact info and one small sentence. *We will conquer your fear together.*

I dropped the cards off to local businesses and paid them a flat fee to keep a stack next to their cash registers.

That's how Evangeline found her. I don't really know the whole Total Exposure story, because I didn't really start that game. I just set it up for Lucinda. She asked me to set up the "game" after Evangeline made contact asking for help getting over her completely debilitating fear of being watched by people. I guess that stemmed from the fact that she was a violin child prodigy and her parents dragged her all over the world as a kid making her perform like a circus dog.

Anyway, Lucinda is a sexual fetish expert in my opinion. She's the one who'll understand what this fight shit is all about.

I call ahead, of course. Sometimes she sees patients at the hospital and she's real busy, but she says she can fit me in, so I go over to her offices and take a seat in her small, private outer lobby to wait for her closed door to open.

You don't knock. She buzzes you in from her office and then you wait until she's ready to see you. Kinda pretentious, but whatever. It's her system and I respect it.

After about five minutes she opens her door, says a few soft words to the patient leaving, and waits for the lobby door to close before she looks at me and says, "Come in, Jordan."

I follow her in, take a seat in a chair in front of her desk and wait for her to sit at her desk.

"So what's going on?" she says.

"You know Augustine and Alexander are back."

"Yup. Are they talking to you yet?"

"Oh, yeah," I say.

"Great," she says, beaming a smile at me.

"Uh, no. Not great. You see… they're having marriage problems and for whatever reason they figure bringing me in is the cure."

"OK," Lucinda says, steepling her fingers under her chin, like she's thinking hard about this. "Not conventional," she says, and lets out a small laugh. "But I don't judge."

"That's not even the half of it," I say. "They have a really weird fetish. One I've never heard of."

"Oh? What is it?"

"It doesn't have a name as far as I know. But they get off on… like… fighting each other."

"Like S&M-type stuff?"

"No. This is the confusing part. There's no top and no bottom. Neither of them is in charge. So it's not S&M and it's got nothing to do with dominant-submissive stuff either. It's just… fighting turns them on. Like he slaps her face, but instead of wanting her to take it, he wants her to hit him back."

"Hmmm," Lucinda says.

"Weird, right?"

"Well… maybe. I think the way it's manifesting is… interesting. I've never heard of that one either. However, their relationship problem-solving—while unorthodox—

is mature. They see a problem and think they have a solution." Lucinda shrugs. "It makes sense."

"But what is it? This *Fight Club* shit?"

"It's not about the fighting, Jordan. It's the push-pull dynamic. The adrenaline and dopamine release that occurs when they feel the excitement of… violence, I guess. Which is slightly disturbing. But I think it falls over on the 'normal' side of things. It's chemical, that's all."

"So listen. The reason they want me is because apparently Alexander is afraid of losing control in these fights. Or possibly had lost control at one point and hurt Augustine. So now he's afraid he'll do it again and he refuses to fuck her. Like at all, Lucinda. Last night, when I was there as their… buffer, I guess… that was the first time he's fucked her in years. And we did her together."

"Hmmm," she says again. "This is a complicated one. But they have come up with a clever defense mechanism to protect each other. So they have a good chance of surviving."

"Should I play this out with them?" I ask.

"Do you want to?"

"No."

"Then why do you need my advice?"

So I explain the part about the building and how I want it back, as well as how Augustine is holding it over my head.

"Sexual blackmail," Lucinda says. "That's not right."

"No," I say. "It sucks."

"So you can't walk away but you don't want to participate either?"

"Correct," I say.

"Well," she says. "It wouldn't be the strangest game we ever played, would it?"

"What?" I smile.

"You came here for help. Do you want it? Or not?"

"You think we should play a game with them? Take their power away and give them what they want at the same time?"

"Why not? I think we can make everyone happy in the end. You get your building, they keep their marriage together, and no one gets hurt."

I agree and we spend the afternoon coming up with their treatment.

But those words echo in my head.

No one gets hurt.

They don't ring true.

Because when you play a game like this everyone gets hurt. It's the only way past the roadblock. It's the only way forward. You have to rip it all apart and put it back together again.

And that always hurts.

My phone is oddly silent the rest of the afternoon. Which can only mean one thing.

I've overplayed my reluctant participant card and now they're angry at me. Gonna wait me out and make me go to them. They've laid all their cards on the table and now it's my turn.

Which is also bullshit. No one puts all their cards on the table. They always hold something back

I leave work early and text Alexander as I walk to my car.

Drinks at my house tonight. Eight-thirty.

The title notification says *delivered*, then changes to *read.* I check the screen one more time as I get in my car, just to see if he'll reply, but he doesn't.

I don't care if he answers me. I don't even care if they show up. If they suddenly decide, *Yeah, we've had enough of Jordan's bullshit,* I'd be pretty OK with that.

But that's not how it's gonna go. You don't upend your whole life for a gamble like this and then suddenly pull out at the last second.

You fuck that bitch hard and come inside her before you finish.

I make three stops on the way, and when I finally get home I make an effort.

Candles. Dozens of them. Pillars, not tapers, because even though I know I own some fancy fucking candelabras, I have no clue where they are at this moment.

Wine for Augustine. Good stuff. A 2007 Sequoia Grove Cambium that comes in a beautiful black bottle with gold lettering.

And of course, a nice whiskey called Hedonism Quindecimus for Alexander and me. Chosen for the label (though it does taste nice too) because it features a very detailed illustration of a dark-haired woman.

And the name. Because… hedonism.

That's pretty much what this whole game is all about. The pursuit of pleasure and sensual self-indulgence.

I change into a fresh suit. Not one I wear to court, even for the most important trials. But one I wear to… things. A gallery opening. A new ballet. The symphony.

Because this is a performance. This entire setup has always been an act, but up until now it has been *their* act.

No more.

I find a playlist called Deep Dark Moods that has about forty songs you can fuck to and stream that through the speakers hidden in the ceiling.

Talking with Lucinda this afternoon has given me a whole new perspective. A new goal to aim for. A new possible outcome.

And, of course, a plan.

A plan, I have found, can fix almost anything in life. A good plan can turn a shitty outcome into an opportunity. And a great plan can turn your whole life around.

This plan might be spectacular.

I take a seat at the desk, one ankle propped up on one knee, and sip from my cut-crystal glass of Hedonism as Portishead pours out of the speakers like smooth waves of velvet.

The gate opens and my eyes are trained on the driveway as I peer through the window. They're late—almost twenty-five minutes—but they show.

I knew they would.

Let the game begin.

"Welcome," I say, watching them come up the front walk through the open front door.

They are holding hands and I catch a slight tightening of their grip as Augustine says, "Sorry we're late. I'm hopeless when it comes to being on time."

Which is a lie. But I don't care. This whole fucking thing is a lie.

"Let me take that," I say, letting my fingertips brush against Augustine's soft skin as I drag the black silk wrap down her arms. Underneath she's wearing a tight red dress. It hugs her hips and breasts like skin. Silk, like the wrap, and soft, I can tell just by looking at it. I admire the choker of diamonds she's wearing around her neck, the matching cuff at her wrist, and… her rings are back. Wedding band and the obscene rock Alexander gave her when they got engaged.

Well… I smile at Alexander as the shawl comes loose and then pivot to hang it in the foyer closet.

"Come in, I hope you had a nice evening. Did you dine out tonight? Or eat in?" I direct my question to Alexander. He's wearing a charcoal-gray suit with a light gray shirt and a deep blue tie. And the first thing that occurs to me is they don't look like a couple. Not that couples should color-coordinate, but there is no cohesion here. A definite line of separation happening.

"We went to that new place over on Stout. The Italian one," he answers.

"Sure," I say. "I've seen it but haven't yet stopped in. Was it all you hoped for?" Now I'm looking at Augustine.

"It was good." She shrugs.

"We weren't going to come," Alexander says.

I smile and wave him into the office. "Then I'm delighted that you did. Wine, Augustine?"

"Yes," she says, rubbing a hand down her arm.

"Are you cold?" I ask, placing my hand on her hip and pulling her into me. I lean down, inhale her scent, then whisper in her ear. "You won't be cold for long. Don't worry."

She backs away from me. Not startled. She won't startle that easy. But put off a little. They both have that vibe to them.

There was an argument tonight. And it was about me.

"I have a special whiskey for us," I say, motioning to the Hedonism Quindecimus as I open the bottle of wine and pour a glass.

Alexander picks up the whiskey bottle and studies the label. No doubt admiring the beautiful woman on the front. Or maybe wondering if it's supposed to remind him of his wife.

"What's this all about?" Alexander says.

This is the kind of game I love. The one where tables are turned. Game pieces scattered on the board. And the rules, such as they were, are thrown out and new ones made up as we go.

"Your invitation, of course."

"You put up a fight all this time and now you're what?" This is Augustine. "Just going to play along?"

Ah. God, I really want to say something like, *Well, playing is my speciality, right?* But what's the point of hinting at things to come? It will come whether I hint or not. "You have something I want. I have something you need. We're making a business deal, that's all."

"That's all?" Alexander says. I slide his glass over to him on the polished bar. He looks down at it, then back up at me.

"And some fun," I say, shrugging. "Don't tell me you two are getting cold feet?" I direct this to Augustine, because she's the instigator of this whole fucked-up plan, not Alexander.

"We know you well," Alexander says. "And when you suddenly come off as over-accommodating it's a flashing red warning sign."

I don't remark on that. Because they're right.

Instead I hold up my glass and say, "To the new us."

And smile.

CHAPTER NINE

I sip, but they don't. And hell, even though the drinks tonight were put out as prop pieces in the game, the Hedonism was a damn good choice.

"Come on, Jordan," Alexander says. "What's this about?"

"It's me, seeing clearly."

"Why the sudden change of heart?" Augustine asks.

I mean… I should be asking them this question, right? Have been asking, actually. So it feels really good to have them on the defensive.

This is where I belong. On this side of things. The instigator. The master.

The light in here is low. Not because I planned it that way with candles, but because several of the wall sconces have burnt-out bulbs that I was too lazy to change over the past few months. So there's only two working behind the desk on the other side of the room, and the chandelier over the wet bar. This lighting complements her the way an illusion tricks the eye. Because it makes her look soft and soft was never something Augustine ever was.

The fight can't be erased. Not by something as fragile as light. So even though her skin is glowing and all her angles are smooth, she is still very hard.

"The change of heart," I say, repeating her question. "Well, let's just say I see this game for what it is. I talked the whole thing through with a friend this afternoon and she gave me the insight I needed."

"Such as?" Alexander asks.

"Look, I get it. You need me to save your marriage. Fine. I'm here to do that. In return"—I look at Augustine now—"you give what I need back."

"The building," she says.

"The building." As if it needs confirming.

"But that was the original deal," she says. "So what's different?"

Perceptive, Augustine. "That," I say, pointing at the camera on the fireplace mantle. "And that one too." I point to another one on a shelf behind the desk. "I have seven in here. So I want a token of faith."

"A video," Alexander huffs. "Didn't you learn your lesson back in LA?"

"Didn't you learn yours?" I quip back.

"Why? To use against us?"

"If I have to," I say, taking a sip of my drink to let that sink in. "I mean… trust, right? It's a hard thing to come by. And I don't trust you. And I'm sure you don't trust me. So… I'm gonna make the movie of us and when you sell me the building, I'll give it back to you. No copies will be made. I'll sign whatever you want to make sure no one ever sees it. But that's my new condition. I need insurance."

They both inhale. Exhale. Look at each other. Look away.

"Fine." Augustine shrugs. Then walks over to the leather couch and sits daintily. Which I love. Because it's an act. Her legs are long and they fold up and tilt to the side a little. A very sexy sitting position, if I do say so. "What do you have in mind tonight?"

"Sex," I say. "What else is there between us?"

She and Alexander exchange another look. These looks, they only come from a couple when they know each other so well, words go unspoken.

Then Alexander says, "There's some rules first."

"Shoot," I say. "Games always have rules."

"First," he says, "she's mine. We're here for us, not you."

"Harsh." I laugh, hand over my heart like I'm wounded. "But OK."

"Second," he says, "you're here for me."

"What's that look like?" I ask. "Seeing as how you're the one out of control and I'm the one here to control you."

"It looks exactly like that. You back off unless I need help."

"You need help?" I ask, squinting my eyes at him. "Or she needs help?"

"It's the same thing," Augustine interjects.

"You two are combative tonight. Which is surprising since you've been pursuing me for weeks. What's that about?" I ask, mimicking Alexander's earlier bluntness.

"It's caution," Alexander says. "This turnaround of yours is unsettling."

"Why? Because you suddenly feel out of control? Well, here's a fucking newsflash for you, Alexander." I change my tone now, the words coming out like a snarl. "You're already out of control. That happened when your wife upended your life and dragged you here. So I can tame you. Shape you into something she can deal with."

"That's not true," Augustine says, voice raised.

"It is true," I say, my eyes locked on Alexander.

"We're still in love," he says back. Meeting my intense gaze.

"Obviously," I say, shrugging with acceptance. "And I've moved on. I've told you that. I'm not interested in the two of you beyond how I can use you to get what I need. So don't forget that." The last few words are directed at Augustine.

"Noted," she whispers. But her body is stiff now. Rigid with tension.

It's dumb. This whole game is dumb. I mean, the animosity in this room is so thick, we're stuck in place. How that translates to life-altering sex, I have no idea.

But it doesn't matter. I'm a defense lawyer. My job is to lie without lying and I do it well. They will get what they came for, even if it's not real, and we'll all come out the other end satisfied the other side got screwed.

I count the seconds of awkward silence and when I get to eight, I've had enough. I unknot the tie at my neck, pull it through my collar with a soft whoosh, and toss it on the ground.

My suit coat comes off next, laid carefully over the back of a chair, and then I'm walking towards her, tossing my platinum cufflinks to the floor and unbuttoning my shirt as I go. I'm getting hard. Harder with each step forward. I don't bother glancing at Alexander, but I know she's watching me because he hasn't moved.

I stand in front of her as I unbutton my shirt. I let it hang open. Let her gaze wander to the lines of cut muscles running across my hips and disappearing inside my pants. They're like an arrow pointing to my cock and there's no way for her to miss this.

She exhales, then drags her eyes away from what she wants and up to what she needs to do to get it.

I take her hand in mine. Stroke it gently. Then place it on my lower stomach. She presses against the tight ripple of muscles. Exhales.

I smile. "Don't move," I say, pointing at her. "And I'm dead fucking serious about that, August."

She swallows. Unsure of exactly what's happening here tonight, but very sure it's something she wants to be part of. Because she nods her affirmation.

I remove her hand and let go. It hangs in the air, like she can't move. Can't do anything without my permission.

God. I'm really good at this mind-fucking these days. These two better have game or they're gonna lose pretty bad.

I turn, unconcerned with what she does with her hand once I can't see it anymore, and give Alexander my full attention.

He's still across the room, arms at his side, mouth slightly open, eyes on me, then darting to her, then back to me as I walk towards him, slipping my shirt down my arms as I approach.

Alexander is like me. Not gay, not even quite bi, but... more than curious. Open, I guess. To whatever feels good.

I feel good. He knows this. We had fun back in LA. Even if it was more about hate and jealousy than anything approaching love or affection.

It's not about hate and jealousy this time. Not about love or affection, either.

It's about greed.

My gaze bores into his. I can almost feel the anger coming off his body. "Relax," I say. "This is gonna be fun."

"I don't—"

But he doesn't get any farther than that, because I lean in, take his face firmly in mine, and kiss him on the lips.

He's muttering protests past my lips but I don't give a fuck. I just push my tongue inside his mouth, grip his head so he can't back away, and kiss him. Open-mouthed. Lots of tongue. Eyes closed. And the second he softens and begins to kiss me back, my hand reaches down for his cock.

He's not hard, but he's close.

I massage him as our kiss becomes less angry and more passionate.

My hands go to his suit coat and slip it down his arms, mouths still locked. Then I back away, smirking at him like I just won a very crucial battle. It's a Bunker Hill kind of win. It's fucking Normandy.

My fingers are on his tie, unknotting it the way I did mine a few minutes ago, only in reverse. It slides through his collar with that familiar sexy sound and goes sailing down to the floor.

"Jordan," Augustine says, behind me.

"Quiet," I say, not bothering to look at her. He's the only thing that matters right now. "Don't fucking move, Augustine. Or this ends, and I do mean *ends.*"

"You think you're in control here, Wells?" Alexander asks me.

"Sure looks that way," I answer back. I'm already unbuttoning his shirt. And he's letting me, so…

I release him from my gaze and look down at his chest as my fingers work the buttons. The muscles beneath are revealed to me four inches at a time and when I get to the waistband of his slacks, I pull the shirt out and finish. Only then do I look back up at him and smile.

I reach for his hand, and he fights me a little, but I grip him hard with both of mine, and then release the cufflink and slip it inside his pocket, my hand purposefully brushing against his now fully erect cock. I do that again with the other hand and this time he puts up no fight.

Jesus. His first surrender comes quick.

Then I have the edges of his collar and I'm slipping his shirt over his shoulders. Letting my fingers graze his skin as I pull the starched cotton down his arms.

His breathing has quickened. It's not heavy and fast like it will be very soon, but there's no denying his heightened arousal now.

I throw his shirt to the floor and we stand there. Two shirtless, half-naked men. Similar build, similar height, similar objectives.

We both want to win. His win is… fuck, I have no idea. I don't really understand these two. But you don't always need to understand a person's motives to catch them off guard and take control of their own game.

"I want to touch you," I say, looking him in the eyes.

Behind me I hear Augustine let out a breath.

"So do it," Alexander says. Impassive. Well, trying to be.

There's only inches separating us, but a moment later those inches are erased. With one step my bare chest presses against his. My face tilts one way, his face the other. My hands on his belt, his hands on mine. The jingle of two sets of hands unbuckling two belts fill the room. And then there's the sound of zippers being released. And breathing, absolutely heavy now, as his hand grips my cock and my hand grips his.

I close my eyes because it feels like the right move. But I open them quick enough to see he did the same.

He's mirroring me. Unable or unwilling to lead when it comes to homoerotic moments. But I got this.

I lean in and kiss him again. This time his mouth is eager. He's waiting for me to guide him, but then he's compliant and malleable. His tongue twisting against mine. The slight stubble around his mouth scratching against the slight stubble of mine.

"You don't get her tonight," I say, still kissing him.

"Fuck you," he whispers back.

"I get you, you get me, she gets us."

He smiles. I can feel it, even though I can't see it. "Sounds good to me."

"It should," I say. "It's what you've always wanted."

"Fuck you," he says again. "I never needed you."

"But yet you're still kissing me." I grab his cock, pulling it out of his boxer briefs.

"Suck me," he says.

"No." I laugh, pulling fully out of the kiss now. "No. You will suck me, Alexander. You will suck me until I come. But I'm not gonna give you that pleasure. Not unless…"

"Unless what?" he asks.

"Not unless you can control yourself."

"That's why you're here," he says back.

"No, wrong again. I'm here for her." I nod my head back towards Augustine, who's been a very good girl while Alexander and I sort through this little power play, because when I look over at her, she truly has not moved. "Now get down on your fucking knees and do your job."

"Fuck you." He laughs.

I do a one-shoulder shrug. "Either you do as I say or you can leave." I look back at Augustine. "You can both leave."

"Do it," Augustine says. "I want to see it, Alexander."

Augustine understands, even though Alexander is still having trouble. I turn my body to look at her properly, because she's slipped her hand under her dress, dragging the silky fabric up to expose the fact that she isn't wearing underwear. Her fingers begin to play with the pink folds of bare skin between her legs.

"You'll make her hot," I say, leaning into Alexander's ear. "You'll drive her crazy. We," I say, stressing the word, "will drive her crazy. Together. And then we can make her scream. Then I'll let you lose a little control. You want that, right?"

He's silent. My whisper is so soft, I'm not even sure he hears me.

"Yes," he finally says. And when I look into his eyes, I see the hunger inside him. A dangerous, voracious appetite that might have slipped into addiction a few years back.

"You want to fuck her?" I whisper. "Hard? Put your hands around her throat? Choke her until she collapses? While your cock is buried deep, *deep* inside her pussy?"

I can hear him swallow.

"Don't you?" I whisper again.

He nods.

"Then get on your knees and pay for the privilege."

I have had many moments I'm not proud of. It comes with the job of game master. Many moments when I have stopped to ask myself existential questions. Who am I and what am I really doing? Am I good? Am I evil?

Alexander drops to his knees, pulling my cock out of my pants, and leans his face in.

This isn't one of them.

Because I do not care.

I grab his hair with both hands. Fist it, and the moment he opens his mouth, I force my way down his throat.

I do not hear his gagging, or his whimpering, or his choking.

Because I do not care.

He needs to learn so many lessons, and tonight's lesson is crucial.

If he wants to dish it out, he needs to learn to take it too.

I press his face up to my stomach. I reach down, grab my balls, and lift them up to his mouth. Make him try to—no. Force him to fit them inside his mouth.

"Look at me," I say, jerking his head as he pulls back to gasp for breath.

Alexander forces his eyes open and lifts them up to meet mine.

I have to wonder what's going through his mind. Is the draw of that power over Augustine so overwhelming that he will put up with… this?

Obviously that answer is yes.

His face is red and blotchy, his eyes watering from the effort of not blinking.

I smile as I bend down, my cock slipping out of his mouth, allowing his stifled gasps of air to turn into long, deep inhalations.

I kiss him on the lips, waiting for him to kiss me back. It takes several seconds, but he finally does. It's lacking the passion he had before I tried to throat-fuck him, but it's an acceptable effort.

"Thank you," I say, whispering the words past his lips. "That was very nice. Should we invite Augustine to join us?"

He backs off my kiss and turns his head to look at his wife.

She is shell-shocked. Eyes wide, hand between her legs pressed flat against her clit. Still now, like she stopped pleasuring herself at some point and forgot what she was doing.

I find that quite adorable.

"Yes or no?" I ask him. "I mean, I'm pretty sure we can have fun without her. So—"

"Yes," Alexander says. "Come here, August."

"Don't move, Augustine," I say. "He's not in charge anymore. Understand?"

"Fuck you," Alexander says. "She's my wife." I grip Alexander's face hard. He resists this time, hands flying up, smacking against my forearms and breaking my hold. "She's *my* fucking wife, Wells."

"She might be," I say. "But I'm her master now."

"Just—" Augustine is standing now. "Just go along, Alexander. This is what you wanted too, remember? We need to find a way forward and this… this might be it. This might be our last chance."

Alexander is near his limit tonight because he gets to his feet. I follow him and back off a few paces to give him the space he needs to think straight. Or… well, not straight. If this guy was thinking straight he'd have never brought his wife over here. Never come to Denver at all.

"Augustine," I say, making a come-here motion with my finger.

She steps forward, slowly. Carefully. Like she might spook Alexander away.

She's here for him. It's so clearly written on her face right now, a little stab of pain shoots through my cold, black heart. She's here to save him from himself. Even if it means she has to temporarily forgive me. Has to look past what I did to them. Has to bow to my sickness and games.

I'm just about to open my mouth and say enough—to stop this before it starts, to save her from herself—when she is close enough to me to take my hand.

Which she does. Carefully. Like I'm dangerous. Like I'm the wild animal in this room, and not her husband. Like I might explode and kill us all.

She looks up into my eyes, her expression going from blank and impassive to soft and seductive. Her hand comes up to my cheek and she smiles as she strokes me.

Lies.

"I understand," she says, holding my gaze for a solid five count before shifting her eyes to Alexander and repeating her decision with more conviction. "I understand."

Lies.

They hurt me. So bad. Because… because I did love her. I wanted her so much. She was my future, not his. She was the love of my life, not his. She was supposed to be with me, not him.

So the lies hurt.

"What should we do now?" she asks. And then, because it has always been her—she has always been the glue that held everything together—she moves between us. One hand flat against my bare chest. The other flat against Alexander's bare chest. And she hums out, "Hmmmm?" Like it's a question. "What should we do now? Should I take off the rest of your clothes?"

She doesn't wait for us. Just turns to her husband and bends down. Her hand finds his cock, an automatic gesture that kills me, for some reason. And then she's slipping his shoes off. Dragging his pants and briefs all the way down his legs until he quietly and obediently steps out of them.

I think I hold my breath the entire time. And when she turns to me I release it in a long, controlled exhale that I try to keep silent.

But she doesn't need to hear the trepidation inside me.

She can see it. She can feel it. She knows me, has known me all this time.

I close my eyes as she grabs my cock now. Slips my shoes off. Drags my pants and briefs down my legs. Then presses her hand flat against the muscle of my thigh, and says, "Step out, Jordan."

Which I do.

And then we—her men—are naked.

And she is not.

Because that's how it's always been, hasn't it?

She has always been the master of us.

Her hand has mine, and when I open my eyes, I see that she has his hand too. She brings them both to her mouth, kisses us at the same time, and then says, "Undress me."

Alexander moves first. Reaching behind her to unzip her dress. Because of course he knows that there's a zipper. He's probably the one who zipped her up earlier this evening. He's probably the one who picked it out of her closet. He's probably the one who bought it for her. Maybe it was a gift? Or something she's been looking at through the glass of a window for months, giving him hints that she'd like it to be hers.

I die. I get lost in their history in that one simple motion of unzipping her dress.

I'm going to lose, I realize.

Lucinda was wrong. I'm not the game master.

Augustine is. Has always been. And always will be the one person who brings me to my knees just like I made Alexander fall to his.

"Jordan," she says, snapping me back to the moment we're sharing. "Undress me."

I pull the dress down, Alexander helping. And it falls to her hips and stays there. She is wearing a black strapless bra that pushes her tits high up on her chest.

"Here," she says, taking our hands and placing them on the bunched-up fabric around her waist. "Pull it down for me, please."

Alexander and I tug—just enough to get it over the curve of her hips—and her dress falls to the floor and forms a silky puddle of red at her feet.

Like blood, I think. The blood we will draw as we attack each other and—

"Touch me," she urges now.

We do. My hand going between her legs, Alexander's up to her breasts. He kisses her while I watch. Unable to think about how he's still claiming her as his while I watch and submit to it.

I look away. Look down at her legs. At my hand. My fingers already pushing inside her. She's not wearing underwear but she is wearing garters and stockings. Black silk stockings. I rub my other hand up and down her leg, feeling the curve of her thigh, the dip behind her knee, the muscles of her calf.

And when I look up again, she is kissing Alexander like she's just as hungry for him as he is for her.

What am I doing here?

Her hand on my head makes me forget to answer my own question. The way she opens her legs for me, inviting me to place my mouth where my hand is already working her clit, blatant and apparent.

I can't *not* obey her.

She is my master, after all.

She is the reason I live. She is the mate of my soul. She is the only woman I've ever really wanted.

I don't care if I have to share her. I don't care that this will end in a matter of weeks. I don't even care that I was set up to lose this game from the very beginning. That my only purpose here is to make their love stronger. To keep their bond together.

My tongue sweeps against her soft, pink folds. Laps at her wet cream. Slips inside her opening as my thumb strums her clit in small circles.

She's breathing heavy now. All three of us are. She is still kissing Alexander. And I am the interloper. The extra one. The intruder.

"Come with me," she says.

I am lost. What the fuck is wrong with me?

But when I look at Alexander, he's lost too. He looks like I feel. He hates me, I realize. Maybe even more than I hate him.

She leads us over to the couch, pointing to it as she looks at Alexander.

He is like her dog now. Her good little dog. Because he lies down, back against the arm. Legs sprawled out across the tufted-leather cushion. She climbs on top of him, hands flat on his chest. Leaning down, her ass in the air acting like my invitation.

I kneel on the couch. Then straddle Alexander's thigh. I lower my hips and drag my balls up his leg as I position myself behind Augustine.

We're going to fuck her. This is nothing new.

What is new is how I feel about it.

How I want to be the one she looks at as we make her come, and not him.

But I am behind her. As usual. And he is in front. Where he belongs.

And this is the saddest thing about what I'm doing.

Because I can't stop.

I can't say no. I won't.

I have never been her master, she has always been mine.

Alexander is already inside her. They are already fucking. She is already moaning, his fingers are already tangled in her hair. His eyes locked on her face as she shows him—and only him—just how much she likes what he's doing.

When I enter her—not her ass, but her pussy—my cock becomes one with Alexander's.

There is no difference between us. There is no separation.

We are one to her.

We are the same.

We are her slaves.

And when we fuck her together—and come with her together—Alexander and I both know we've lost.

Because she doesn't want him, or me. She wants us.

The climax is loud. We are slick with sweat by the time we're exhausted. She has come from two men spilling out of her pussy. It drips onto Alexander's leg. She collapses against his chest and he hugs her.

And there's no room for me now.

None at all.

CHAPTER TEN

"So… what's going on? You're having some kind of existential crisis?"

"What?" I ask, looking at Darrel. His face is dead serious. Like this is the most important thing about this conversation we're having. Which it isn't. Because we're discussing my father taking the day off and me picking up a case of his this afternoon. "Why the hell would you ask me that?"

"Why are you getting so defensive?"

"I'm not getting defensive. I'm just wondering where you're getting the impression I'm having some kind of identity crisis when we're talking about my father."

And I'm wondering that because I haven't said much to Darrel about this whole A&A Bartos tragedy-in-the-making. He's kinda judge-y and to be quite honest, I'm not in the mood for his self-righteous judgment.

"It's an easy leap," Darrel says.

"No, it's not. So what? I'm having a little fling with some exes. That has absolutely nothing to do with my father."

"Your father being… sick," he corrects me. His gaze locked on mine. His eyes completely devoid of emotion. Some people find that glare intimidating but I know it's just his resting bitch-face.

"We don't know he's sick. He just went in for some tests. The results haven't even come back yet."

Darrel raises his eyebrows at me. That look says, *Come on, asshole. Don't bullshit me.*

"He just needs a day off," I say. I start that sentence with conviction but by the time I finish, even I'm not buying it. "And anyway, I just need you to tell me what I need to juggle to keep this day on track, that's all."

He stares at me. Silent. Slowly nodding. Then he tosses a file onto my desk and says, "It's just a deposition. But it's not here. It's down at the offices of Sawyer, Brand, and Farfield."

"Thanks," I say, picking up the folder and opening it. Pretending to be absorbed in legalese.

"Is there anything else I can help you with that Eileen should be doing?"

"Fuck you," I say.

"She's worried about her job."

"She is not," I say, snapping at him. "She knows I just like you to handle my schedule because of the games."

Well, she's not really in on the game part. But my days are fluid and Darrel is the one I want handling that kind of thing, not her.

"Don't you have shit to do?" I ask him. I'm getting annoyed and I hate being around people when I'm annoyed because I turn into an asshole. And turning into an asshole feels good in the moment, but I always regret it the next moment, and then I feel worse… so yeah. He needs to go.

"Yup," Darrel says, taking the hint. "Call me if you need anything."

He walks out and it's only when the door closes that I remember to call out, "Thank you!" to him.

Not that he's some whiny bitch who needs praise, or anything. I sigh. It just makes me feel like less of an asshole.

Then my phone buzzes and Eileen says, "Jordan?"

"Yeah?"

"Alexander Bartos is here to see you."

"Fuuuuck." I sigh. "Send him in."

A few seconds later the door opens and Alexander appears. Smiling. Happy. Holding a bag. "Brought you lunch."

I lean back in my chair and appreciate this unexpected change of events. "You brought me lunch?"

"Yeah, it's lunchtime," he says, pointing to the clock on my wall. "Just some burgers from the Mile High Cafe. And I figured…" He sighs, then drops into one of the chairs in front of my desk. "I figured we'd better talk this shit out before we get together again."

"Talk what shit out?" I ask, reaching for the bag. Because I skipped breakfast this morning after my mother called to ask if I'd handle my father's two o'clock.

"You know. How you fit in."

I laugh. "I don't fit in, Alexander. And I completely understand that, so don't sweat it. I'm fine."

He narrows his eyes at me. Taking a moment to digest what I just said. While I open up my burger and take a bit. Then he says, "I don't get you."

"What don't you get?" I ask, mouth still full.

"How you're so fucking clueless."

"About what?" I feel that itch of annoyance creeping back up my spine.

"About what we're doing."

"We're playing a game," I say, dragging a napkin across my mouth. "And it's gonna be over in a couple weeks, so…" I shrug. "I'm not gonna think too hard about it."

"Is that what you think? That this is a game?"

"This is a game. You two came here to use me to fix yourselves—"

"Fuck you," Alexander snaps. "Just fuck you, Jordan. Do you really think we'd upend our lives… that I'd quit my fucking job and move halfway across the country just to play a stupid game with you for a few weeks?"

"You guys want me to save your marriage. And that's pretty fuckin' stupid to start with. Because if you need a third to fall back in love—"

"We don't need you," he snaps.

"The hell—" I laugh.

"We want *you*."

Which makes me pause and take a breath.

"But I feel like we've been talking that to death, ya know? I'm not here to talk you into the idea of us."

"Then why are you here?"

He does this little half-shrug. Which is kinda fucking cute. I guess. Even though Alexander is the oldest, he's always had a boyish kind of charm. And it's still there. "Just… you know. To try to get to know you again."

"You never knew me back then, either."

"Fair," he says. "Fair point. I…" He sighs and takes a moment. Like he needs to collect his thoughts. "I just figured you were…" Another shrug.

"Forgettable?" I ask.

"Ah… no," he says, pointing his finger at me. "Not that. Just temporary, I guess. I mean it started out as summers and holidays, so when you moved to LA for law school it kinda… it kinda threw us off balance, ya know?"

"Not really," I say. "Because Ixion was already out by then."

"Right," Alexander says. "So yeah. I was wrong. You didn't throw us off balance. You…" He pauses again to stare at me. "You balanced shit out pretty perfectly."

I grin. And then I chuckle. I don't laugh, not on the outside, because I'm cool like that. Because I have always known this and he has always resisted, and yeah. Here this motherfucker is telling me I was right.

"Fine," Alexander says. "I'll say it. You had me at hello. You complete me, Jordan."

Then I do laugh.

We both laugh.

"You're a dumbass."

He shrugs. He likes to do that these days, I guess. A very give-no-fucks gesture. "Guilty." But then he sits up in his chair and leans forward on my desk. "But it's true, OK? I've missed you too. Maybe not *you* you. Because I don't really know you. Never did and still don't. But what you brought to the relationship."

"What did I bring?" I ask, acutely aware that this comes off as needy.

But he doesn't laugh at me and I appreciate that. "Excitement, ya know? Back then you were a challenge. Something I had to deal with. And I'll be honest with you, I didn't have a lot of challenges before Augustine came into my life."

Which makes me realize I never knew him either. Still don't. So I say, "Who were you then? And who are you now?"

He looks down at his hands. It's a moment of insecurity, I think. "Bartos, you know what that is, right?"

"Yeah," I say. "Vaguely, at least."

"A brand. Not so much in North America, but in Central Europe the name Bartos is synonymous with wealth." Then he pauses to think for a moment. "And poverty. And wealth again. It was kind of a cycle with my family back in Hungary. That part of the story is long and sad. Lots of losses and few wins. But later, in the last half of the twentieth century, our luck changed and my father held a patent used for sound recording. Later he had more. Mostly film-making tech. And we were suddenly very, very wealthy. This was right around the time I was born, so I never knew the old version of my family. I grew up on a large, rambling country estate in Luxembourg. I went to school in the US, then university at Oxford, then back to the US for grad school. Which is how I ended up in LA sitting on that board when I met Augustine."

"Hmm," I say, picturing all this. Picturing little tow-headed Alexander running around in fancy European kid clothes playing croquet or something. "Interesting."

"I was a privileged brat."

"I can see that," I say. Then I smile. Because actually, even though I always knew Alexander came from money, he never acted like he came from money. He was always just one of those strange artists. Of course, broke strange artists don't live in Westwood lofts. It was kind of a shithole back then, but still. Three bedrooms, three baths, three thousand square feet.

He hit the trifecta with that place and we all knew it, even if we never talked about it.

"So I had it easy," Alexander says, slipping into some kind of fake Hungarian accent. Although… is it fake? Maybe this part of him, the part I know, is fake?

He's watching me try to figure this out.

"I had it easy," he repeats, now in perfect English. "Augustine was my first real challenge in life. I fell in love with her the moment we met. She was in film school, I had just finished grad school the year before and was a consultant for an academic organization that gave out grants for film students. It wasn't fair, I knew that. To dangle that money in front of Augustine. She needed it and…" He shrugs again. But this time he's frowning. "I needed her."

"And so she took your bait," I say.

"Ixion was just her friend. He was no threat, I knew that immediately. They were partners, they had business plans, and he was not at all interested in a sexual relationship with her until…"

"Until I came along," I finish for him.

"Yeah, well. You changed everything, Jordan. I knew it the moment we met as well. You were competition. So I had two choices, right? Let you in or chase you away. If I let you in, we share her. If I chase you away, I lose her. So what could I do?"

His accent is back and for some reason it throws me. It tilts my world a little. Because I don't know Alexander Bartos with the thick Hungarian accent. I have no fucking idea who this guy is.

And he's staring at me. Daring me to ask him this question. "What do you want?"

"Her," he says. "So simple, right? I just want her."

"And she wants me."

"She doesn't want you. She needs you, Jordan."

I think about this for a few moments. "Your family," I say. "They're dangerous people?"

"All people are dangerous."

"Right," I whisper.

"You're dangerous people too, so don't worry about that."

I wonder how much he knows about me? How unbalanced is this relationship?

"We're here to figure this out and we need you to do it." His English is perfect again.

Fucking. Weird.

"So what do ya say? You in?"

"I mean… I said I was. I don't know why you guys keep asking me this. I want the building so I'm game, OK? I have no objections to what we're doing."

"Do you love her?" he asks.

"No," I say. And it surprises me even more than it surprises him. Because it's true. "No," I say again. "I don't love her. I don't know what I feel about her, but I don't love her. I mean, I care about her. Of course." I let out an uncomfortable laugh. "I care about her. I want her to be happy. Whatever that looks like." And then I shrug. I don't know what else to do. What else to say.

"Sounds a lot like love to me," he says.

"I guess. I dunno. OK, look, I'll be straight with you. It feels like we've maybe… turned a corner here. Right?"

He nods. Tacitly agreeing.

"So…" I sigh. Trying to put these feelings into words. "Yeah."

He smiles, then huffs out a little laugh.

"I mean… OK. I like it. I don't know why it's so hard for me to admit that, but it is. I thought we were over and turns out… we're not. So… I'm just… a little bit… surprised about that, I guess."

"We like it too. And yeah, we're just as surprised as you are."

"You are? But… you came here for me, right?" I get this sick feeling in my stomach when he hesitates. This sick, sick feeling that I'm missing something here. Something very important and life changing.

"We did," he says. And even though that's the right answer, that feeling doesn't go away.

"Don't fuck with me, Alex. OK? Please? If you want revenge or whatever, fine. Get it however you need to get it. But just… don't lie about this part."

He stares at me for a few moments. Like there's a million things running through his mind. Like he's wondering... should I keep lying? Or should I come clean?

"Feelings don't lie, Jordan. So, no we're not lying. It's just… nice, I think. It's nice."

"Which part?"

He shrugs. "All of you. I mean, you were kinda hostile last week."

"So were you."

"Fair. But it does feel like we've turned a corner. I agree. The dynamic started out a bit… muddled. As was the objective."

"Because you guys are making that part up, aren't you?"

"It's clear now," he says. Not really answering my question. "It's clear you still love her."

"I'm not in this to steal her, OK?"

"You can't steal her, Jordan. She's not a thing."

"I get that," I say, irritated. "I'm not insinuating she is. I'm just saying… if you guys don't make it, don't blame me. It's not me. I don't want her. I don't want you. I need that fucking building and you two just happen to have it."

"She needs that building too. That's why she's playing this game."

"What?"

"She has plans for it."

"Like what?" I ask.

"She can tell you herself. That's the reason I came here today. We're going to look at it tonight. Do you wanna come?"

"To the building?" I ask.

"Yes." He nods. "Meet us there at eight. Unless you wanna come for dinner." He winks at me.

I squint back at him with suspicious, narrowed eyes. He's so fucking confusing. I mean, what the fuck was this visit about? Not lunch. Not some dude-bonding time, either. It's just another move in the game.

"No? OK. Then enjoy your burger and we'll see you tonight."

He stands up, buttons his suit coat, and then waits.

What the fuck is he waiting for?

"See you then?" I say. Trying to make him go away. God, this guy. I fucking hate how he makes me so uncomfortable. I fucking hate how easy it is for him to do it, too.

"Unless you want me to stay for something else," he adds.

"Like what?" I ask, my irritation totally showing now.

"Some fun, of course."

"You're not even into it, so don't play like you are."

"Last night I was pretty into it."

"Yeah," I say, remembering how he fucked her. Just… took her. Like she's his.

Then he's walking around my desk and I can't help myself, I lean back in my chair. Which is the wrong move, I realize, because when he reaches me, he bends at the waist, places one hand on either arm of my chair, boxing me in place, and leans forward to kiss my mouth.

I kiss him back and feel myself grow hard.

I'm wondering who the fuck he is as my tongue slips against his. He picks up one hand and slides it behind my neck, pulling me close to him. Into him. And then his other hand is on my belt, unbuckling it. Unbuttoning my pants. Pulling out my shirt. Unzipping me.

And finally, he's holding me in his firm grip.

We stop kissing as he begins to pump my cock. Just hold our lips close to each other. Breathing heavy. Looking at each other.

He doesn't get on his knees. In fact, I instinctively understand that there is no possible scenario where he gives me another blow job. I just know that. Can feel this power vibe radiating off him like… steam.

"I'll keep going if you don't mind coming in my hand and me wiping it on your shirt," he says.

Fuuuck.

"But if you don't have another suit here at work, I'd advise you to say no. Because I'm gonna make it messy."

I just… stare at him.

Which makes him smile, then chuckle, then laugh, and finally… he lets go of me and steps back.

"Tonight," he says. "You can show me what you love about this building of yours. Why you need it so bad."

And then he double-slaps my cheek. Not hard, but not soft either. And walks out of my office. Leaving me there with a hard cock sticking up out of my pants, a rumpled shirt, and desire for him I didn't have when he walked in.

I'll give him one thing. I don't exactly forget about my father, but Alexander's visit definitely pushes it to the back burner of my mind for the rest of the afternoon.

I give the deposition my full attention because it's my job. Plus, it's my father's client and letting him down in any way when he's so busy with other issues just isn't an option.

But that's the last appointment of the day and by the time I go back to the office, answer a few emails, and then head home to waste time before I meet up with Alexander and Augustine, I'm… fucking nervous.

I'm nervous to walk back into the club. I'm nervous to see it with them. I'm anxious about what comes next.

I was in there a couple months back. Broke in with Darrel because Augustine has owned it for over a year and a half now and the place has been sitting empty. I was dying to know what was happening in there.

That was a big fat nothing. The whole place was still… our place. The Turning Point Club. Except there was plastic sheeting over things and layers of dust.

God, why did Bric ever sell it?

Why didn't I just buy it back then?

And how long have Augustine and Alexander been planning this little reunion?

I pour myself a drink, sit on the couch in my office bedroom, and think about Alexander's visit today.

I wonder what Augustine was doing while he was with me?

My mind wanders with possibilities. Strange ideas pop into my head. Things that have more to do with that Hungarian accent Alexander sprang on me this afternoon. Things that have to do with our life back in LA. The memories of a too-hot summer, and the broken AC, and the sweaty sex.

And of course, how I fucked it all up with that little plot to use Ixion to break Augustine and Alexander apart.

It's weird too. Because I was the one with the fixation on cameras and filming people. Watching them in private moments. But Ix was the one who took that and made it into a career.

First with film school. And he and Augustine had a little production company going. They made shorts, ya know? The artsy kind you enter into film festivals.

And even though he dabbled in our little quasi-quad we had that summer, he was always the watcher. Always the one behind the camera.

I knew Augustine loved him, just in a different way. He was always the most important member of our… team. They were best friends. By that time Ixion and I had gone separate ways, but we kept in touch and he was the one who invited me into his tight-knit world.

I was the one who pulled it all apart. Found that unraveling thread and pulled on it until there was nothing but a chaotic pile of what once was.

I set him up. I set up the cameras, and the date with Augustine. I set up the sex. I set up Alexander. Had him walk in. Set up the reveal. The fact that the whole thing was on film. All of it.

And Augustine freaked the fuck out.

Not on me, like she should've. Would've, had she known back then I was the one responsible.

But Ixion.

I tore them apart with my bullshit.

What I did was a felony and if Ixion hadn't just sucked it up and took the charges Augustine filed against him…

if he had told her it was me... well, let's just say I wouldn't be a lawyer right now. I'd have done some time, probably.

She only dropped the charges on Ix because his whole family died in that car crash. He was in jail when it happened—his dad flatly refused to bail him out. Ixion always did have that bad-boy persona and I guess this was the last straw. So he was left in jail to await the trial.

Then he missed the funeral.

Then she dropped the charges.

Ixion's mother, father and little sister died thinking he was a pervert who makes sex tapes with unsuspecting women.

But he wasn't.

I was.

I gulp down my drink, then get up and pour myself another. I gulp that down too, standing at the front window, looking out onto the elaborately landscaped front garden bathed in the soft glow of expensive landscape lighting.

He was never the same after that.

None of us were. Not even Alexander was the same and it had nothing to do with him at all. He married August, they moved on as a couple, and... whatever. They split up, and got back together, and a part of me knows all of that was my fault.

They know it too. That's why they're here. They need to fit all those fucked-up pieces into the fucked-up puzzle we created back in LA so they can move on.

You'd think I'd have learned my lesson.

You'd think I'd change my ways.

You'd think running these games would be the last thing I'd get involved in.

Of course, you'd be wrong.

Because deep down inside I am one sick motherfucker.

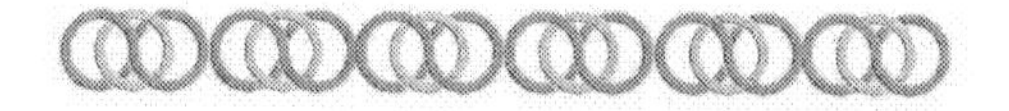

At seven-fifty-two I'm standing before the revolving doors at the front of the old Turning Point Club, unable to reconcile what I'm seeing.

The building is an old historical brownstone with an elaborate facade. Six stories in all, and all the windows are tall.

They remind me of the windows on the front of my empty mansion and I let my mind wander for a moment, wondering if they were built at the same time, or maybe they are even…

My phone dings a text.

I take it out of my pocket and read the screen. It's from Alexander and it says, *Come inside.*

I look back at the revolving doors. At the soft glow of light that filters through the frosted glass. The windows are shuttered, like this is another night, in that other life when the weekends here were filled with people dressed in black and white and the shuttered windows were a sign that there was fun to be had inside.

Private fun. Hot, sweaty, sexy fun.

I take a deep breath, straighten the lapel of my black tuxedo—because the Club always did have a dress code—and then step into the cramped compartment of the revolving door and push.

I could hear the music outside. It was part of the reason I hesitated. Got lost in the memories of how it used to be. Felt that little pang of ache that started two winters ago when I was last here and never seemed to fade away.

It's just… music, ya know. Background noise. And if this was real, and not an illusion, it would be accompanied by the clink and clatter of silverware on china, and platters of food being served in the White Room restaurant off to my left. And the tink of cut-crystal glasses filled with Macallan, or Hine Triomphe, or Hennessy Paradis Impérial in the Black Room bar off to my right.

All the wives would be dressed in white or silver, and all the men in black tie.

And Bric would be there. I glance over at the bar. Picture him talking to people. Picture people hanging on his every word. The gregarious laughter that would always come after. The side looks he would throw at me, or Quin, or Smith, maybe. Which makes me look up to the second-floor balcony overlooking the Black Room and the grand lobby, where you'd always find Smith. Watching. Waiting. This was before Chella. Back when he was still weird. Back when things were fun for me.

I was new at the Club. Just became a member a few weeks before. It was Lucinda's birthday and there was a party for her. She chose me to take her downstairs and share her with her husband.

It was a fun night.

But it was more than fun. It felt like… like after all the bullshit in LA I'd finally found my place in the world. A place where what we wanted out of marriage and sexual partnerships wasn't discouraged.

Where we could all just be ourselves.

"I'm so glad you came," Augustine says.

And it's like she knows. Because she's wearing a long silver gown. I have to take a deep breath. Have to stop the memory of those long-gone nights from becoming too real.

"It looks the same," I say, noticing Alexander now. He's sitting at a booth near the window. The same booth Nadia and I sat in when I first mentioned her to Bric. First *gave* her to Bric, is probably more accurate.

They're not married yet, but they will be soon.

"Come," Augustine says. "Sit." She waves a hand to Alexander's booth. My booth. You can't see outside because of the shutters, but I know… I know people are looking at this place right now, asking themselves, *Is it open again?*

I walk over to Alexander and slide into the booth opposite him.

He stands, waits for Augustine to get in the booth, then sits again.

I let out a long breath as we stare at each other.

"This is it, huh?" Augustine asks.

I nod. "Sorta."

"What do you want to do with it?" Alexander asks.

"What do you mean? I want to fucking open it back up."

"Just like this?"Augustine asks.

"Yeah. Just like this."

"Why?" Alexander asks.

"Because I miss it. We all miss it."

"Who's we?" Alexander asks.

"Me." I laugh. "Everyone who used to be a member."

"OK," Augustine says.

"Why are you doing this?" I ask.

"We want to understand," Alexander says.

"We want to know why it's so important to you," Augustine adds.

I shrug. "It's just a place where I can… be me."

"You can be you lots of places," Augustine says.

"Not really," I say, wishing this was all real and not some fake setup to trap me in this game they're playing. I get up and go over to the bar without saying anything, grab a highball glass off the shelf, and take down the bottle of Hennessy.

"When did you clean it all up?" I ask, pouring my drink.

"Been working on it for the last few weeks," Augustine says.

I turn to face them, walk round to the other side of the bar, then lean back on it as I sip my drink. "I broke in here about two months ago and it was a fucking mess."

"Yes, we know," Alexander says, standing up, then offering his hand to Augustine. "That's how we knew you were ready." He holds her hand as he leads her over to me. Places her on my left, then goes behind the bar and, as I tilt my body towards Augustine, I see him reach for two more glasses and pour each of them their own Hennessy.

"Ready?" I laugh. "For what?"

"For us," Augustine says.

"I'm ready for all this to go back to the way it was," I say.

Alexander returns to stand in between us, hands his wife her drink, then raises his glass. "To the way it was," he says, making a toast.

Augustine clinks his glass, but I don't. I just drink down my cognac.

"So what's so special about it?" Augustine asks. "This could be any restaurant and bar."

"It's not," I say.

"Then show us," Alexander says. "Show us what you want, Jordan. What you need."

"Why? So you can convince me I don't need it?"

"So we can give it to you," August offers.

But I don't think I can. I really don't think I can. "I don't want to see this place empty. It's… sad."

"Then tell us about it," Alexander says. "Tell what you liked. Tell us what you need, Jordan."

I look around, my eyes darting to the stairs that lead up to the second floor elevators. "That," I say, pointing to the landing with my glass. "That's how you get upstairs to the upper floors. And that," I say, pointing up to Smith's balcony. "That's the bar where Smith used to sit and watch."

I glance at Alexander. He's nodding his head.

"And over there," I say, pointing to the White Room. "That was the public face of the Club. The White Room restaurant. Anyone could come here to eat in the White Room. But this place, the Black Room bar, it was strictly for members. Before I was a member I'd come to the White Room and watch them."

God, it fucking hurts to picture it. Because it was exciting, and fun, and real.

"I was so close back then."

"So close to what?" Augustine asks.

"Being invited in, of course." I smile as I down the rest of my drink. Remembering back that night of Lucinda's birthday was my very first private party. "And over there, behind the stairs, there's elevators back there. They take you to the basement. That's where all the fun stuff happened."

"Take us down there," Augustine says, picking up my hand to hold it. "Take us down there and show us what you need, Jordan."

For a moment I wonder… do they have people down there? Is there a party happening and I just don't know it yet? Is this some kind of surprise?

But no. There's not.

"You own it," I say. "You've been down there so you know exactly what it look like."

"We don't care what it looks like," Alexander says. "We want to know what it *feels* like."

I hesitate. Unsure if I can. Will it make everything worse? Or will it bring me relief?

"I dunno," I say. "Maybe I should just go."

But that thought barely makes it past my lips. Because Alexander's mouth is on mine. Kissing me as Augustine moves in, pressing her body against mine. Her lips coming up to join us.

I close my eyes and pretend.

Pretend this is real, even though I know it isn't.

Pretend that I will go downstairs with them and there will be people waiting. Women, naked. Some marked up with fluorescent paint, letting me know they're into plurality. Letting me know I'm welcome to join in.

And Augustine would be painted up like that too, if this was real. She'd be naked, and Alexander and I would stay dressed in our black and white tuxes all fucking night. Our zippers down, cocks sticking out, as the night morphs from the mundane into a carnal delight.

"Come on," Augustine says. "Show us what you need."

CHAPTER ELEVEN

The elevators in the back of the grand lobby are how you enter the *real* Turning Point Club. These elevators only go down one level. There's stairs somewhere. Fire regulations say there have to be stairs. And I'm pretty sure there's a service elevator for staff and whatever.

But guests use *these* elevators.

The same black and white marble floor tiles carry over from the lobby. The cab front is one-of-a-kind art deco metal etching with sharp, zigzagged lines that criss and cross each other as they climb up the silver plate and expand into a geometric sunburst at the top.

It's erotic in its own right and just stepping inside—just hearing the tap, tap, tap of our shoes on the chevron-pattern floor—is enough to make me feel better.

Just a little bit.

The doors close and the three of us stare at each other in the soft white light from the two wall sconces.

And then the doors open and we step out…

The strobing black lights make the white paint glow on her body. Her black mask hides her face from us, revealing only the desire in her eyes. The music is pounding, pulsing, and the place is packed, moans and screams of pleasure in progress weaving their way past bodies and echoing through the hallways.

Everywhere there are men in tuxedos. Fully dressed with zippers down, cocks spilling out of their pants and into hands, or mouths, or whatever. All the women are naked. Some with white paint to signal they want more than a one-on-one, some not, indicating they're there only for their husbands.

The room where we belong is off to my left. A smallish space with three walls so people can watch us as we take her. There's a white vinyl bed with a cage underneath it and when we lead her over to it, she climbs onto the mattress and crawls towards the top with her ass in the air.

Bric smiles at Quin, and Quin smiles at me, and—

It's empty and quiet. The black walls look garish and stupid with the overhead lights on. The white vinyl chairs and couches look aged and overused. The tiled marble floor is scuffed, and the magic is gone. Faded away or left behind, I'm not sure.

"Let's go," I say, backing away, then turning on my heel to head back into the elevator.

"No," Augustine says, grabbing a hold of my arm. "Tell us, Jordan. Tell us *why* you need this place."

"It's not the same," I say. "Let's just go."

"Then tell us what's missing."

"I can't," I say, suddenly angry. "I can't, OK? It's stupid. It's fucking pointless. There aren't enough words in the English language to compare these empty hallways and silent rooms to what it was."

"Why are you so upset?" she asks.

I glance at Alexander, but apparently he's sitting this discussion out. Because he just stares back at me and keeps quiet.

"I'm upset," I say, trying to figure it out as I talk. "I'm upset because this place was fucking perfect. And I'm sorry I came down here with you because it ruins all the memories of what it was."

"Why was it perfect?" Augustine prods.

I just shake my head in response.

"Why can't you just admit it?"

"Admit what?" I say, too loudly.

"That you need more than one person to love, Jordan. Jesus, are you that clueless?"

"I don't need to love anyone. Nothing that happened down here for me had anything to do with love. It was sex. That's it. Just dirty sex."

Alexander wanders down the hallway, peeking into the various scene rooms, leaving Augustine and I to our argument. I watch him stop at a set of stairs that lead up to a party space. A place for people to congregate on white couches and peer down into the scene room below through the glass floor.

"Dirty sex. And that's it?"

"That's it," I say, still watching Alexander, who moves on, away from the stairs, not curious enough to go up there. Or maybe he knows. Hell, they've owned this place for a long time now. There's no way they never came down here to check it out.

"So it had nothing to do with you hating who you are?"

A laugh bursts out unexpectedly. "Hating… fuck off, August. I don't hate myself."

"No?" she asks. "Are you sure about that?"

"Look, I'm not having this discussion with you. I'm not—"

"You're just going to run away? Again? Like you always do?"

"When did I ever run away?"

She shrugs, then leans back against the wall. I glance down the hallway, but Alexander is gone. Slipped into a room or another hallway while I wasn't looking. "You left Colorado for California when you were eighteen."

"I went to Stanford. That's not running away."

"And you didn't come back for law school," she continues, like she didn't hear me.

"Because UCLA is a great fucking school."

"And Ixion was there."

"So?"

"So you loved him, and you followed him, and then…" She gives me a small, weak smile. "And then you met me. And it was all set for you, wasn't it, Jordan?"

"What the fuck are you talking about?"

"Him. And me. And Alexander. And you. You," she says, "are a deviant. And you never wanted to admit it. So you just followed him. The boy you fell in love with as a young man."

"I don't fucking love him that way."

"Not anymore," Augustine says. "But that's only because you're not his type. That woman he loves now? Evangeline? She's his type. He's never going to share her with you."

I want to yell at her. Tell her to shut up. Fucking wrap my hands around her neck and choke her into silence.

"And you always knew that. He was never into you that way. Oh, he loved you, but not the way you loved him. That's why Ixion saved your ass, then walked away and never looked back."

"In case you didn't notice, that's what I did as well."

"No," she says. "You got stuck in the past. You want something you never had, Jordan. Him. That's the only explanation for why you're being so difficult about this offer we're making you."

"You want me to moderate your husband's dark side, Augustine. That's it."

"That's it?" she says. "And you know this how? Because you asked us what we wanted and we told you? Or because you're making it up as you pine for this fantasy club? This place didn't make you happy. The people you shared it with made you happy."

"Yeah," I say. "That's true. And you two weren't there."

"No. We came first."

She and I stare at each other for a few seconds.

"Hey," Alexander says, peeking his head out of one of the scene rooms. "Come down here."

"Fuck that, I'm leaving."

"Fuck you, Jordan," Augustine spits. "Fuck you if you walk out again!"

I step back, stunned by her sudden venom and anger.

"We're tired of this shit. We came here in good faith to try to get you back—"

"You came here so I could help you—"

"Just fucking listen to me!" She screams it. "Just shut your fucking mouth and listen to me for once! Can't you see what's happening? How can you be so clueless?"

I huff out a laugh. "Enlighten me, then, Augustine. Tell me what I'm missing."

She glares at me. Points her finger in my face. "You're missing everything. You see nothing but lies. You see nothing but your made-up past, and you project that onto us like we're the ones responsible."

I swat her hand away, sick and tired of all the drama and bullshit that comes off these two like a sick, thick fog.

"I'm not responsible for your happiness, Augustine. I'm not your cure, or your Band-Aid, or your fucking scapegoat. What you two have—the good, the bad, all of it—has nothing to do with me. This is a fucking business decision. This is a fucking contract. This is a fucking…" I stumble for words, unable to find another analogy.

"A fucking *game*," she spits. "You've been playing games your whole life. That's all you know how to do. That's all you are. One long game. That's all you've ever been and ever will be, because you're too goddamned afraid to see the truth standing right in front of you."

"The truth in front of me?" I laugh. "The truth in front of me is one sad, lost woman who chose the wrong man years ago and now she regrets it and wants a second chance."

Oh, yeah. Even I feel that burn.

Augustine stands still. Silent. Her eyes welling up like she might start crying.

I turn away, done with this shit. Ready to get the fuck away from her. From both of them.

"If you walk out on us one more time, Jordan," Alexander says, "don't ever fucking come back. Because you know what? I'm tired of you treating my wife like she's some piece of shit under your shoe." He steps fully into the hallway now. Jaw set and clenched. Eyes locked on mine. Mouth even and without any hint of affection. "She never did anything to you. She wasn't the one who lied and manipulated people. She wasn't the one who ruined everything. She's here to save us, yeah. OK. Fine. But she's here to save you too."

"Save me?" I laugh so loud I almost startle myself. The guffaw is unexpectedly real. "What a fucking joke. I don't need saving. Like… what fucking world do you two live in? What fucking reality? I didn't ask you to come here. I didn't ask you to give me another chance. I didn't do any of this. I walked away and left you two alone. Just like you wanted. And now that I'm happy, and things are going great—"

"Going *great*?" Alexander belts out an incredulous laugh.

"—you two want to steal my satisfaction. Like fucking leeches. Like blood-sucking vampires."

"Is that what you think?" he asks. His words a soft, angry whisper as he slowly walks towards me. Stops directly in front of me. "How did you get this far?"

"What?"

"In life, Jordan. I mean… it's sad, man. Fucking sad."

"Stop it, Alexander. Leave him alone."

I glance over at Augustine. Narrowing my eyes at her. Something… something is happening here and I'm not sure what.

"No," Alexander says. "No," he says again. "I'm done playing his game. Jordan needs to know."

"Know what?" I ask. "What the fuck are you talking about?"

Then Augustine is in between us. Her hands on my arms. Her body pressing into me. Face tilted up as I glance down at her, eyes wide and begging. "Can you just… just trust me for once?"

I redirect my stare back to Alexander. "What do I need to know?"

"That we love you," Augustine says quickly. Almost urgently.

Which is so funny—but sad at the same time. So I don't bother laughing.

"We love you, Jordan. That's why we're here. We were young back in LA. We were messing around with sex, and feelings, and there were a lot of emotions involved. It wasn't you who did that, ya know? It wasn't you."

"No?" I ask. "Who was it then?"

"It was the sick fuck living inside you," Alexander growls.

"Stop it!" Augustine says, whirling around to face him. Her back presses against my chest now. Like she's a shield trying to protect me. "Just stop it, Alexander. You're making things worse."

"Am I?" he asks. And it doesn't come off as sarcastic or anything. Just like a real question.

"Don't walk away," Augustine says. "Please. Just show us what you need. What you want. What makes you…" She shrugs. "Happy. And all you've been talking about—the only reason you're doing this with us—is this place. This stupid building is what makes you happy. So help us give you that."

"You could give me that by selling me the fucking building," I say. It's mean. I know it's mean. She's being real, and emotional, and putting herself out there and I'm being sarcastic, and shallow, and self-absorbed. But it's true, isn't it? If all she wants is to make me happy, then sell me the fucking building and stop this game. "This isn't my game," I say, trying to explain. "You guys started this. How did you even know that I wanted this building? Like… how did you even come to own it?"

They share a nervous glance. But it's quick. Too quick for me to decipher it properly.

"It's the darkness," Alexander says.

Which redirects my attention. "What?"

"Inside you. That's the draw of this place. It's not the building. It's the darkness you keep collared and leashed. This place is just a symbol, Jordan. Where you felt safe. Where you could let it out of the cage."

Is it, I wonder? Is that why I have all these thoughts and feelings about Turning Point Club?

"At least you can admit it," Augustine says. And then she shrugs. "That's a really good first step."

I start thinking about that one game I organized with Finn and his girl, Issy. How I tricked her into thinking she wasn't playing a game, but of course, she was. It just wasn't her game. She had a pretty specific sex club fantasy of being watched by strangers. But then I turned the whole thing upside down and yeah. I had other things in mind for that game and she was just the vehicle I used to get where I needed to go.

But I played it off using the sex club thing as an excuse. A way to back out.

But was it? Just an excuse?

"Right?" Augustine says, pulling me back out of my thoughts.

"Admit it," I say, repeating her question. "What did I admit? I didn't admit to anything. That was Alexander's overactive imagination."

She lets out a huff of air, like I'm exasperating her. "Do you or don't you have a fucking dark side?"

"Why are you getting pissy with me?"

"Just… do you?"

I shrug. "Maybe. I guess. I mean, fucking more than one person at a time isn't really dark. But whatever. I like it."

"You like it with strangers, Jordan." This is Alexander. "That's the key with you, ya know."

I stare at him for a second. "I like it with you guys too."

"Of course you do," Augustine says. "Because we're where it all began, right?"

I have to hold in a laugh. "No. I was always into it. It's just… you guys… you two and Ixion were the first I did it with more than once."

"So why is that?" she asks.

"Because I fell in love with you, Augustine. You *know* that."

"But not me?" Alexander says.

"No. Not you. You were just there."

"Like Ixion," he adds.

"No, not like him, either. He was… he was *always* there."

"Do you think he'd bring Evangeline here?" Alexander asks. "If you opened the place back up? I mean, is that what you're after? Them, with you. So you could have him?"

"He's not like that. At *all*," I say, stressing the word. "We're just not like that."

"But you'd want it that way. So maybe deep down your new obsession with this building, with reopening the Club, it's all related back to what he never offered up?"

I pause. Considering this.

Is it?

"The Club has been closed for over a year, yet you just started getting interested in it recently. Why is that, Jordan?"

I stare at Alexander. Wondering if that's true. Was I over it? And then did I get drawn back in by the reappearance of Ix?

"I have no grand delusion that Ix, Evangeline, and I will become partners, you guys. None. That's not what this is about."

"Then what's it about?" Alexander asks.

Augustine shoots him a look. Like she wants him to shut up but he won't.

"I just want a place to go." It's lame. Even I know it's lame. But it's true. That's really all I want. "A place that's familiar. Where I know people. Where I'm not judged or made to feel… dark." I shoot a look at Alexander. "Where I can be me and not feel weird, I guess."

"Like… a home," Augustine says.

"Sure. I guess."

"Where you can have multiple partners and never commit," Alexander offers.

"Goddammit, Alexander," Augustine snaps.

"What?" he says. All exasperated with her annoyance. "I'm just following his fucking lead."

"It's not about multiple partners," I say, thinking it through as I ignore their disagreement on how to 'handle' me. "It's just… expectations are set from the beginning. There's no room for mistakes. Everyone knows how to play the game. Everyone understands the rules."

"So it's safe," Alexander says.

"Yeah." I shrug. "So what?"

"Well, it's funny." He laughs. "That perfectly describes what you didn't have with us in LA. There were no rules. There were no expectations."

"But there were plenty of consequences," I add.

"Not for you," he quips back. "Ixion took your fall back there."

"And I'm fucking sorry about that, OK? I told him that. I've apologized to you two. I'm fucking sorry. And if you're still pissed off about it, then why are you here?"

"Just fucking tell him, August. For fuck's sake. Can't you see he's never going to figure it out on his own?"

"Tell me what? Figure what out?"

Alexander opens his mouth to speak. And I swear to God, I have a moment of panic that he's gonna say something… I dunno. *Bad.*

But then Augustine beats him to it and says, "That we love you. That we're here because we love you, and care about you, and want you in our lives again. And… we're worried about you."

"OK." I laugh. Because this is stupid. "That's the third goddamned reason you've given me so far. First," I say, holding up one finger, "you told me that you guys needed me to save your marriage. Because of Augustine. She missed me, and even though you don't miss me"—I look at Alexander—"you love her and I was the only hope you had of keeping her. Then," I say, ticking off another finger, "you tell me he's dangerous or some bullshit like that. He can't control himself. But oddly enough, none of that has come through in the sex we've had so far. And now," I say, holding up a third finger. "Now you're both in love with me. So which one is it?" I stare at them. First her, then him, then back to her. "Which of these is true and which are lies?"

Augustine opens her mouth to speak, but she stutters."I… we… listen, you just…"

"We love you," Alexander says. "I mean, for fuck's sake, Wells. No one would put up with your bullshit if they didn't love you."

"I find your answer somewhat hard to believe."

"Whatever," he says. "I'm sick of explaining myself to you."

"It's just not… coming off as authentic," I say. I look at Augustine and shrug. "Sorry. It's just not."

"Did we ever tell you why we split up?"

"Alexander," Augustine interrupts. "No."

"Shh," he says. "Quiet. We did this your way and it's not working. So it's my turn now." He directs his attention to me now. "Did we?"

"You know you didn't," I say. "Nothing beyond, 'She was bored. I wasn't enough for her.' You know, your typical bullshit lies."

He points his finger at me. "For the sake of everyone's sanity, I'm gonna go ahead and ignore your standard sarcastic defense mechanism. It was about…" He looks at Augustine. "What? Four years ago?"

"Three and a half," she says back.

"Fine. Three and a half years ago."

I laugh. "That honeymoon didn't last long."

"We were in our old Westwood neighborhood for a theatre production at UCLA. And we were walking past the old apartment. I sold it shortly after you left. We moved into a house in Silver Lake. Anyway, I said…" And he stops to look at Augustine. "I said, 'I miss those days.' And she said, 'You hated those days. You were never into sharing.' And I said, 'I don't like sharing you, that's true. It turned me into a jealous asshole. But I always knew he never wanted you. Not really, so I didn't care. I always knew I could outlast him. I always knew he'd leave eventually. I always knew he'd get sick of you and move on.'"

"Ouch," I say, looking over at August. She's not looking at either of us.

"And she said—"

"And I said," Augustine says, cutting him off. "I said, 'Well, he was the only thing holding us together.'"

Alexander nods. "That's what she said. It took me a few more months before I really thought about that. And another year to admit it was true. And another year after that to finally realize… I mean, I don't know *how* I love you, Jordan. But this," he says, waving his hand between himself and his wife. "This only works if we're all here. Sometimes things come in threes. And… you know, I lied to her that day in Westwood. I lied. I liked it. I stayed because it felt good. I wasn't jealous of you because… because I knew it wasn't the attraction of a magnet. There was no push-pull of opposite poles. It wasn't salt. That's sodium chloride, right? Table salt. Those two things are held together by positive and negative charges. But simply adding water can undo those bonds. We were never that fragile. Not while we were three. We were like… triple bonds. Those rare things in nature that require more than one or two but three to be stable. And that makes us stronger, I think. That makes us… unique. And no, it's not common. And no, it's not for everyone. But we can't help who we are. We can't change our inherent natural qualities. We can't be two." He pauses. Draws in a long breath. "We simply cannot be two. We either exist alone or all three of us together. That's just the way it is."

I glance over at Augustine. Who has gone absolutely still. Like this is the first time she's hearing this little speech from her husband as well.

"So fuck it. We lied. OK? We lied. We're here for you and we're using this building to get what we want because…" He shrugs. "It just doesn't work any other way. Do I wish I could have a wife to myself? I dunno.

Maybe? I really don't know. Because that's never going to be an option if I stay with Augustine. It's just not an option. And I love her. And you too, I guess. I don't know. But I'm certainly willing to give it a try if you are."

I've been holding my breath and it comes out in a soft, low exhale. "Well, I admit. I didn't expect *that.*"

Augustine takes Alexander's hand and places it on her cheek. She smiles up at him like he's her God. And then she turns to me and says, "I'd like to try too."

There's two things running through my brain right now. One. They're full of shit. Something else is going on and this was just… I dunno. His way of distracting me. And two…

God, that's hard to admit.

Two.

They're serious. We had something good, we lost it, and now we want it back. I mean… besides Ixion. Because what we had included him, regardless of what he thinks about it.

I don't want to be cynical Jordan anymore. Life is short. That's one thing I've learned since we fell apart. One thing that really hit home these past few months when the games took a dark turn.

I mean… I had a US Senator *killed* a few months ago.

He deserved it. He was a total piece of shit. And in my defense, I did wait for him to make his choice before I made the call.

But who do I think I am? Really. Who the fuck gave me the right to kill a man for another person's vengeance?

Chella never asked me to do it. She didn't complain after, but…

"Jordan," Augustine says, pushing herself so close to me, I can practically hear her heart beating fast. "Just… give it a try. You have nothing to lose."

Is that true?

"Oh, for fuck's sake," Alexander says, getting irritated with my indecision. "Forget it."

He turns to walk away but I grab his arm and say, "Wait."

"Why?" he growls.

"I'm just… I've got a lot on my mind. And you two, man. You came out of the fuckin' blue and I don't know what to think about that."

"So stop thinking," he says, shrugging me off.

Which might be good advice. Maybe the best advice.

So I reach for him again. I pull him towards me with a hard jerk. And when he takes those two steps forward and comes into our space, I lean in and kiss him.

For a moment he hesitates. And a jolt of realization courses through me. A sick feeling in my gut that this was all a lie. All a plot to… to… something.

But then his mouth softens and his lips react, and we're kissing.

And relief floods through me so thoroughly. My muscles respond with some kind of endorphin or adrenaline rush. Filling me with heat, and a weird feeling that defies description.

Augustine's hand is at my cock. My eyes are closed, my mouth still kissing Alexander. But I know she reaches for him too because he groans.

"Wait, wait," I mumble. Not wanting to stop but…

"What now?" Alexander asks.

"Be right back."

I don't wait for them to answer. I know I'm on Alexander's last nerve tonight. But I don't care. I kinda like pissing him off. Besides, he doesn't have to wait for me. She's *his* wife.

I turn the corner in the hallway and find the control room door. This is where—predictably—all the controls are for the basement. Lights, music, sound effects. Yeah, I didn't realize that last part was a thing. But when I broke in here a couple months ago I went snooping around and that's when I found the control room. And the moaning soundtrack.

It's actually more than moaning. There's whispers too. Male voices mostly, but some female. His voice is demanding. Hers, accommodating.

And I don't recall this being a thing, since it was probably played under the thumping music and there were plenty of real-life men whispering commands and plenty of real-life women giving in to them as they moaned, but it's fucking hot.

And I want them to hear it. If they can't experience the real Club, then I can give them a little sample at least.

I flip the switch on the master control panel and choose the last track combination I played for music.

I might not care if Alexander starts without me, but I don't want to miss anything either.

Then I find the small jar of white paint, grab two paintbrushes, and flip the main lights out and the black lights on as I exit.

It's… porny as fuck.

And just admitting that to myself makes me smile. Because whatever.

When I make my way back to the hallway where I left them, Alexander has Augustine pushed up against the wall. His hand has lifted up the hem of her dress and he's caressing her thigh as he kisses her neck.

Her eyes are closed. Her mouth is open. Her sweet, plump lips are moving just a little. Like they need a job to do. Like she wants to put them on his cock and suck.

That's the real magic of plural sex. The woman can't help it. She's being stimulated in so many ways and in so many places she just… wants things. Wants to fill herself up in every way possible.

I set the paint and brushes down on a small table and slip in next to them. One hand on Alexander's waist, the other reaching for Augustine's breast. My mouth finds hers and I fulfill the need she didn't even realize she had. Her tongue sweeps across my lips. Probing and twisting. Alexander has one palm flat against the wall, boxing Augustine in on one side. The other… it reaches behind me and grips the back of my neck.

He pushes us closer. Asking us to do more.

I'm in a giving mood, so…

I rip her dress down the front.

She gasps. He laughs.

I just grin and keep going. Shredding it down the middle, ripping it free, pulling her strapless bra down as I whisper in her ear, "I'll take you shopping for a new one tomorrow."

Alexander helps me get her naked. Off comes the bra and panties—we leave the stockings and garters on.

And then I back away, admiring her body in the black light. Getting hard just listening to the whispers and moans filtering through under the thumping music.

And I get the paint.

Alexander's grin is worth all the fighting and effort we've put into this new adventure. Totally worth it.

He takes a brush when I offer it, winks at his wife, dips the end in the white paint, and draws a circle around her nipple.

She glows in the dark now.

Yeah, this… this is what I've missed.

I dip my brush in the paint too and draw a line starting between her breasts, right down to her shaved pussy. She closes her eyes when I tickle her clit. Moaning. Real moaning.

And Alexander, right on cue, begins to whisper in her ear. "You like that? You want more? You like us both, don't you. You want us both inside you."

And she responds with hums, and groans, and "Yeses."

I hand the paint to Alexander, then reach for him. Grabbing his cock through his pants. He looks at me, startled, but then he just grins lazily and resumes his painting.

I unzip his pants. My hand pushing its way inside the opening, grabbing at his hard cock. He's not wearing any underwear and that makes me want to kiss him. Because he's kinda perfect. For me.

No. For us.

I pull him out. That's how the men stay in the Club. Fully dressed in black tie, zippers open with protruding hard cocks sticking out.

"Fuck," he says, my hand already pumping him.

Augustine is paying attention because she reaches for my zipper. Her hand pushing its way inside my pants and then a smile as she realizes I am also bare.

Perfect for her. For us.

Her fingertips fold over my shaft as she pulls me out and begins to stroke me. Gently at first, but when I reach up and twist her nipple, she grips me hard. And I, in turn, squeeze Alexander.

We are a chain reaction.

We are a chain reaction of lust, and longing, and labored breathing. We unfold, then fold again, reshaping what we thought we were, who we thought we were, into what we will become.

We are a chain reaction of past into present into future. A single bond becoming double, becoming triple, becoming…

Complete.

We are sweaty skin under our starched shirts, and white, wet paint marring and scarring the blackness of our tuxedo lapels as Augustine writhes against our collective touch and I think…

I think…

There is no mask on this woman when there should be a mask. And there's no other bodies pressing against us when there should be other bodies. And there's no scene being played out in the rooms nearby or at the end of the hallway or… anywhere.

It's just us.

In this forgotten playground of carnal desire and delight.

It's just us.

In this old building basement that, when devoid of the magic of lights, and music, and sound effects, is just that.

An old building basement.

I say, "Let's go."

And there's confusion. A little bit. And questions painted on their dark faces like the white stripe I painted down Augustine's torso.

She is naked, save for her stockings and garters. But I take off my coat, then my shirt—as Alexander watches me with curiosity and fascination. His eyes on the muscles of my stomach. His hands automatically reaching out to touch.

I place my shirt over her shoulders and she in turn slips her arms into it. I button her up and reach for Alexander's pants, tugging on his belt buckle then slipping it through the loops as he continues to watch, and touch, and whisper things like, "Yeah… Yeah."

I reach around Augustine's waist, cinching the belt tight against my shirt she's now wearing. Then I take Alexander's coat off him, missing his touch when he has to pull away to let the silky lining of the sleeves slip past his arms.

But his fingertips resume their exploration of me. Softly sliding down the muscles of my back as I drape the coat over Augustine's shoulders and then she slips her arms in, and they slide down the warm silky lining where his arms used to be, and I swear to God, she sighs.

I put my suit coat back on. And now we are a mismatch of clothes. I have no shirt and Alexander has no coat, and she has no dress.

"Let's go," I say again, turning away but grabbing her hand as I do that, so I can lead her.

We enter the elevator, leaving the basement behind.

Empty, but still loud with music and whispers.

Dark, but still lit up with black light.

Lonely, because when we leave, when we get to the lobby and exit through the frosted glass revolving door, there's no one left to play the games this building used to play.

Alexander lingers behind, locking the Club back up with his key. And I lead Augustine to the car parked in what used to be the valet.

We hear a gasp come from off to the right.

Chella's Tea Room.

Groups of women sitting in the outdoor tables stop sipping their drinks, their mugs and cups paused at their lips as they see something they haven't seen in a very long time.

Three people exiting the place where they used to play.

"Shit," Augustine says, acutely aware that she is a woman guilty of carnal pleasures. And we, her men, are missing a coat and a shirt. And the paint. Oh, I bet they miss the paint and all the pleasure it guaranteed them once upon a time. "They're looking at us. They know."

And then Alexander is there, opening her door. Eyes locked on mine as she gets into the passenger seat of his sporty black German car.

He says, "Let them look."

And then he closes her up inside and grins at me.

I nod. Grinning back.

Let them look.

We fucked hard last night.

And softly too.

It was heated and passionate. But there must be some truth to Alexander's dark side, because he did come very close to crossing a few lines.

The choking came first. Then the slapping. First her ass. Which made her moan for more. Then her face, which made her come.

But I stepped in. Unsure how much truth there was to that lie they told.

Late that night, or maybe it was early this morning, we took a shower. I finished first, exhausted and ready to climb between the sheets of their bed.

Our bed?

I heard them whispering in the master bathroom. I didn't catch it all. I was too tired to care. But I heard her say something like, "This doesn't change anything."

I drifted off trying to understand her. What she meant by that.

Didn't change anything between them? Maybe?

So they are having marriage issues after all.

Then sleep took me away and I no longer cared. The perfect night was over and I was happy.

I'm meeting Evangeline at the Mile High Cafe across the street from the Capitol building. She called me at work this morning and asked to have lunch. I wasn't sure why she'd want to have lunch with me, but the only obvious reason is Ixion. And I'm always in for a conversation about Ixion.

She already has a table in the back when I walk in and push my way past the crowd of courthouse people waiting for their takeaway sandwiches or hoping for a place to sit and relax. I see her first, already heading to the back, when she lifts her hand to wave at me.

I don't know her that well. Not really. I mean, I know more than I should. More than most. Because I was in charge of running her Total Exposure game a few months back. So I know her issues, and her fears, and that she overcame them. I know she loves Ixion the way I do. I know he loves her back, probably not the way he loves me.

She is thin, but shapely. Dark hair and bright eyes. And she's a very talented violinist. Was once a child prodigy who toured the world playing for celebrities, and royalty, and CEO's.

I know she's sensitive, and artistic, and even though Ixion put all her shattered pieces back together, she has leftover chips and cracks.

He's careful with her.

So I'm careful with her too.

I smile as I approach her table, unsure how to greet her properly—a handshake like we're business partners, when we're not. Or a kiss to the cheek like we're old friends, when we're not.

I opt for neither. Neutrality. And just take my seat. "How are you?" I ask.

"Well," she says. "Very well, actually."

"And Ixion?" I ask, my voice low and throaty when I say his name.

"Also well." She smiles at me again, but this time it's tight. "But that's what I want to talk to you about."

"Oh?" I ask, feeling a little sick that the thought of them having issues… excites me.

Things with Augustine and Alexander seem to be working out—at the very least, they're starting to make sense—and the only thing missing now is the fourth piece of the quasi-quad we once had.

And that's so inappropriate.

"Tell me what's on your mind," I say, shaking my head at the waitress who appears to ask if I want to order something. Evangeline isn't eating, so I decide this won't be an eating lunch. Just a talking lunch.

"I know you're his best friend—"

Which makes me laugh. And makes her pause.

"What?"

"Well." I chuckle. "We were. Once. But…"

"No," she says, reaching across the table to take my hand in both of hers. "You are." And then her tight smile becomes warm again as she lets go and leans back in her chair. "Trust me."

I want to ask all the questions about that. Like… *Does he talk about me? Does he tell you about our childhood? Or mention anything about what we were to each other back in LA? Or what I did to him to make him disappear? Make him hate me?*

But that's not why she's here and anyway, she's going to tell me something, even if it's not any of that. And something is enough for now.

"It's about the house," she says. "The mansion next to the Botanic Gardens where we played our game."

"Oh," I say. "Yeah. He came by a few days ago wanting to know more about it."

"You didn't tell him, did you?"

"Tell him what?" I ask. "I don't know anything. I mean… I live there now. It's mine. But I bought it in foreclosure and the bank, you know. They're not chatty. They give you a price and you pay it or don't. That's about all I know about that place."

She sighs with relief. "Good. Good. Well, I did some digging on my own. Lucinda helped me…"

I lose my train of thought for a moment when she mentions Lucinda's name. Fucking Lucinda. She's been in my life a lot since I joined the Club a few years ago. She was the first one to accept me. The night of her birthday Bric threw a party and when the Club throws a party for a member's wife, it's… a pretty sexy affair.

I fucked her with her husband that night. And everyone watched.

God… last night I thought I was over it. But thinking about what I had, and what I don't have now… it brings it all back to me. Makes it fresh again.

I'm kind of a sick fuck.

"… so what do you think?"

"I'm sorry?"

"About telling him?"

"OK, explain this to me again? Sorry, I wandered."

She smiles and huffs out some air. A little bit frustrated with me, but not much. "We figured out who the house belonged to."

"OK."

"That family in the pictures that were all over the house."

"Makes sense," I say.

"Well, the house was in foreclosure, but it's the reason why it was in foreclosure that makes me hesitate."

"Oh," I say. "OK."

"They died."

"They died?"

"Yes. In a horrific car crash last summer on their way home from Grand Lake."

"Oh…" And then I realize why she doesn't want me to tell Ixion. "Shit."

"Apparently there was a freak thunderstorm and they—"

"No," I say, waving my hand. "I don't need to know." Because I don't want to picture them slipping off the side of a mountain. A whole fucking family. "The baby," I say. "The house had a nursery."

"I know," Evangeline says. "It's horrible. Just… horrible. I was so obsessed with them when I was in the house last winter. And it felt like they were still living there, ya know? Like they were gonna come home any minute. I had pictured them all on vacation. Perhaps they didn't like the cold, I remember thinking. And they spend their winters in the south of France. But I was wrong."

I take a deep breath and let it out. "No, he doesn't need to know this."

"I'm glad you feel the same way. I mean, I love the house, Jordan. Love it. Ix mentioned that you're living there, and I'm so glad it's not empty. Because I was gonna ask him to try to talk you into selling it to us. But now… I just don't like the idea of Ixion living in a home where an entire family died like…"

"Like his did," I say, finishing for her when she doesn't.

She nods and swallows. "Yeah. Like his did."

I don't know why this news upsets me so much. It's not like I knew that family. But I can't go home. I just can't walk in there knowing. And even though I live in the office, I can't stand to think about the empty nursery upstairs. Or the little girl's room. Or the teenage boy.

Or the master bedroom.

The only thing worse than a whole family dying is one of them surviving.

So I drive. I just leave work and get in my car and drive. And the phone is ringing and buzzing texts at me, so I turn it off.

I don't know why. I really don't understand what's happening to me. All I know is that I don't want to talk to anyone.

I just drive north on I-25. Just keep going past Fort Collins, past the Wyoming border. Past Cheyenne. And when I get to Casper, I head west for some unknown reason. West towards… something. I dunno why. I just keep driving. Then I'm going north. The darkness is all around me as I head towards Thermopolis. And then all the little towns on Highway 20 start popping up on road signs.

Kirby.

Winchester.

Worland.

Washakie Ten.

Washakie Ten. I say it over and over in my head. Washakie Ten, where Ixion landed last year and hid out in a tiny cabin. Washakie Ten, a place I knew once. Washakie Ten…

I know where the dirt road is. How? I have no idea. But I find it. Against all odds in the dark. I find it. And I turn off the main road and head deeper into the woods. The pine trees tower over the road like giants, obscuring the stars and the moon.

The cabin is dark and looks so much smaller than I remember. I turn off the car and just sit there, the ticking of a hot engine the only sound.

And I remember…

We're going hunting, he'd said. Turkeys or deer, I don't really remember. It didn't matter because we weren't there to hunt. We were there to fix me.

I close my eyes and pinch the bridge of my nose. Not now. Why am I here? Why now? After all these years? Why now?

She was tall, and older. Not old, probably not eighteen because that would've been so much worse… but older than me. I was twelve. And she was very pretty. Very pretty. I remember thinking, Why is she wearing that dress in the woods? You can't hunt in a dress.

And maybe she read minds or maybe I didn't think it, I said it out loud. Because she gave me a sad, sad smile.

And she said, "I'm yours for the weekend, Jordan. Your father paid for me. Do you know what that means?"

And I did. I knew.

But he'd left by then. Some excuse that he needed to go to the store and pick up milk or whatever. So we were alone. And she took off her clothes, and then she took off mine too.

"We're going to play a game," she said. "A dirty little game."

And I don't know what my face looked like in that moment, but I remember how I felt. And I remember what she said next. "Would you like to play a dirty little game with me?"

I get out of the car and walk up to the front porch. My hand reaches for the door and finds it unlocked.

I don't know what I expect. Leftover filth from squatters maybe. Because that year I turned twelve was the last time I came up to Washakie Ten.

But what I find is a perfectly neat and tidy hunting cabin. Even in the faint light of the moon coming through the front windows I can tell people have been here recently.

Does he rent it out? Do they—my parents—come here? I try to picture my father bringing my mother here for a long weekend and find I can't.

The light switch is right where I expect it to be. My fingers flick it on and I see the old, worn, leather couch. A couch that lived in my father's home office until I was… what? Seven? Eight, maybe?

We just stood there. And she took my hand and placed my fingertips on her breast. She smiled. I remember her smiling as she cupped my hand around the firm mound of flesh. She squeezed it for me because I didn't know what to do.

"He knows your secret," she said.

"What secret?" I asked.

"That you like boys, Jordan."

I squinted my eyes. Trying to figure out what that meant.

"But girls are who you're supposed to like."

"I like girls," I said. I remember my throat tightening up. Making it hard to swallow. Like there were rocks in there or something.

"Of course you do," she said. "Of course you do," she repeated. Her mouth angling in to mine until our lips touched.

I kissed her back.

The bedroom—my bedroom—looks the same too. A raw log bed with a small child-sized mattress is pushed up against the wall. I liked it against the wall because the wall was comforting to me. I liked to press my back up against it. The patchwork quilt my mother bought from a local Indian reservation when I was small still acts as a bedspread. The pillow cases are navy blue…

When it was all over I just looked at her. At her hair. Spilling out onto the pillow. It's golden, and long, and soft. I touched it a lot that night. Played with it as we played our dirty little game. As she touched me, and caressed me, and fondled me.

"Where did you come from?" I remember asking when it was over and the morning sunlight was spilling through the window.

And she said… and she said… "He keeps me."

And I didn't know what that meant back then.

But I do now.

CHAPTER THIRTEEN

I think some fathers do things like this. They hire a prostitute for their teenage son and turn it into a big deal. A tradition.

Sick fucks. Rich fucks. Fucks like my father.

But this is so much worse now that I think back on the experience. What she said… *To fix me.* To make sure I like girls, in other words.

I think I blocked it out because one, I just didn't understand it. Oh, I knew I was there to have sex with her. That wasn't the part I misunderstood. But I did like girls. I still do like girls. I just… liked Ixion too. And two, because my father… I fucking worshipped him.

Still do. I love him.

But he did that to me. Said those things to her.

Fix me.

I fall into the couch cushions, exhausted from the long drive. Wondering if my mother knew.

Loving men is confusing because you have your best bros. Like me and Ix. And I love him. I'd do anything for him. Any. Thing. But it's not supposed to go any farther than that. You're not supposed to crave his body, or his attention, or his touch.

And to be clear, Ixion and I were never like that. He's not into the bi stuff like I am. Sure, we shared Augustine a few times, but that's all it was. A share.

I'm not looking for a man, I'm looking for a man and a woman. I'm looking for what we had back in LA. And now that what happened here is reemerging, I have to ask myself—did my father make me this way? Was this formative experience what made me who I am today?

A man who is unable to find satisfaction outside a plural relationship?

Her game was clever for the time. I mean, no one even blinks at a blindfold these days, but back then? It was super kinky.

Put this over my eyes and take me out to the woods, Jordan. Tie me up and smack me with this twig. I will pretend to cry and you can rip my dress off. Touch me anywhere you want. Touch yourself, too.

Did my father tell her to do that? Or did she make it up? What kind of teenage girl knows how to do that shit?

A very badly abused one, Jordan.

She scared me. I remember thinking that. I remember taking her out to the woods, blindfolded so I had to hold her hand and tell her to step carefully, and tying her to the tree like she told me to.

But after that… after that I just froze.

It didn't make any sense. None of it made any fucking sense to me. What was I supposed to do with her?

And the things she said to me. I know now that it's just playing, right? Games. Dirty talk. Things that make you hot.

But I had never had sex before. Barely even masturbated. I wasn't thinking about sex with Ixion. I was thinking about football and Christmas. I was thinking we had fun last summer and this winter his family was taking me skiing with them in Aspen. I was thinking in one more year we'd be in middle school and then after that we'd get our driver's permits, and then… I dunno. Whatever. We'd have fun, like we always did. And it would all feel pretty good because it always did. That's why we were best friends in the first place.

I didn't get it, I just knew it was wrong. More wrong than any confusing feelings I ever had for Ixion.

And I felt shame.

It was a dirty little game and that's exactly what it felt like.

Dirty.

Being alone with this girl made me feel dirty. Filled me with shame.

And when I got back home Ixion asked me, "How was the hunt? Did you tag a deer?"

So it must've been deer. Because I remember staring at his face as he asked me that.

And I said, "No. It wasn't that kind of hunting trip."

And somehow he could tell something was wrong. He knew. He felt it, or I was acting weird, or I dunno. He just knew.

I remember sitting up in my room at my desk, just staring out my window. There was a pine tree just outside. Ix and I used to climb it when we were small. I fell off once and broke my arm. He was there for that. Went with me to the hospital. Signed a great big red X on my cast.

And he was there this night too. He decided to sleep over. And I know now that it was because he was worried about me. He didn't want to leave me alone. I had these moods I went though sometimes. And therapists I'd go talk to. But until that night when I tied that rope around the tree branch, slipped it around my neck, and was about to jump off and end everything for good… I didn't understand why my parents made me see therapists.

You're not supposed to like boys.

But I did like him.

He stopped me. He saved me.

How could I not love him for that?

And then he saved me again when I fucked everyone over in LA. He swooped in like the best friend he was and pulled me out of the flames.

What would my dad have thought of me if Ixion wasn't there?

Should I care? Since it was him, and that weekend with that girl who made me who I am today? Is that why I can't manage a normal relationship with a woman? Is that why all the world's a game to me?

Is that why… is that why I had Chella's father killed and never even blinked?

Was it him—*my* father—who I really wanted dead?

The sound of a slamming car door wakes me up. Sunlight is shining through the windows. Boots thud on the old wooden porch as they approach the door.

Then knocking. "Jordan?"

It's Ixion.

"Come in," I croak out, my throat still dry from sleep.

He opens the door and peeks his head in cautiously. "Hey," he says, coming inside and then closing the door behind him.

"How'd you know I was here?"

"Augustine called, looking for you. And then Evangeline mentioned she had lunch with you yesterday so I got Darrel to track your company car. What the fuck are you doing up here?"

He walks across the room and takes a seat in the chair opposite the couch. I sit up, rubbing a hand down my face to wake myself up.

"Did she tell you?" I ask. "About the house?"

"What house?"

"My house."

"What about it?"

"She found out what happened to the family who used to live there."

"OK." He waits for me to explain, so when I don't, he continues. "Well, what happened to them?"

"We decided not to tell you."

This make him grin, rake his fingers through his tousled hair, and then chuckle. "So why bring it up?"

"Because that's why I'm here, I guess."

He gets serious then. Props his foot on his opposite knee to wait me out.

"You remember that time I came up here with my dad to go… hunting?"

"Which time?" he asks. But I can tell by the expression on his face, just after the words come out of his mouth, that he knows which time.

I nod. Then swallow hard and lean forward, head in my hands, and stare at my feet. I still have my shoes on. I still have my suit on. I must look like a total fucking mess. "It wasn't hunting."

"No?" Ix asks. Cautious now. "I mean… I figured something bad happened since, you know, what you did that night I stayed over was kinda… drastic."

I nod again, then lift my head a little so I can look at him from underneath my tumbling hair. "He had a prostitute waiting for me up here."

"What?"

"Yeah. He left me with her and then… then she told me why. He wanted her to fix me."

Ixion shakes his head, not understanding. "Fix you? How?"

"I guess… I guess he was afraid I was gay?" I shrug.

"What?" Ix whispers.

"Yeah. So he hired this girl. She was young, like probably not even eighteen. He hired her to… I dunno."

"Fuck you, obviously," Ix offers.

"No," I say. "I mean, yeah. That. But it was more than that, Ixion. It was weird. Very, very weird shit. Like BDSM shit."

He just stares at me. "Why? I mean, OK. I've heard of this kind of shit from other kids when we were in high school. Other boys who got this kind of gift. A kinda get-it-out-of-your-system type thing. But you were like…"

"Twelve," I say. "I was twelve."

"That's the year…" But then he pauses. Thinks about that for a second.

And I wonder, is he putting two and two together now? Because twelve… that's the year I started using the cameras to find out people's secrets. That's the year I talked him into doing it too. That's the year we figured out his father had a mistress and his mother knew about it, and… yeah. Kinda shattered his perfect illusion of love and family.

"That's the year I got weird," I finish for him.

"That's why you wanted to kill yourself that night?"

I shrug. Because I… guess?

"Are you gay?" he asks.

"I guess bi counts as gay. I dunno. I like women too. I don't really want to fuck dudes. I just want more. I don't know why, Ixion. It just makes me…"

"Happy?" he asks.

I nod. "Yeah. I just like it. I like not being the only one. I like sharing. I like… *kink*." That last word. *Kink*. It comes out soft and low. Like I'm ashamed, which is stupid. Because everyone already knows all this about me. There's not a person in my inner circle who doesn't know what I am. What I like. What I want.

Even my father knows this. Somewhere along the way he just… accepted it. It's not a secret. I'm not hiding who I am.

So why is it so hard to admit it out loud to my best friend?

"I hate your father," Ixion finally says, breaking my silence.

"I don't," I say.

Ixion huffs out a laugh, then sighs. A long, loud exhale. "He was always mean to me. Trying to make me stop being your friend. He was a dick. And when I got out of jail, after… you know… he called me up one day."

"What?"

"Yeah," Ix says. "It was the usual sorry-for-your-loss bullshit. But then right before he hung up, he said, 'You killed them. That stunt you pulled in LA was what killed them.'"

"Jesus Christ," I say. "I'm so fucking sorry, Ix."

"Wasn't you. I mean"—he huffs—"I blamed you, I did. But it wasn't you who killed them. And it wasn't me either. And you know what?" He stares at me. His eyes glassy. Blurry. Bloodshot like he's been up all night driving out here.

"What?"

"Fuck him. Fuck my dad, ya know? He cheated on my mom all those years. And fuck her too."

"Don't do that," I say. "Don't—"

"Don't what?" He laughs. "Don't tell the truth? I mean, look. I took the fall for you because I didn't want your life to get screwed up over such a stupid mistake. And fuck Augustine for believing I was the one who made that sex tape. And fuck Alexander too. Fuck everyone. They all thought I was that kind of guy, ya know? The kind of guy who'd make a sex tape of his friend to ruin her life."

"You're not, I am."

"Yeah," he says. "You are that guy." And then he laughs. "But I don't even care that you're that guy. Because deep down we're all fucked up. Everyone is fucked up. We all have secrets. We all have shame. We all have something in the past we're not proud of. We all make mistakes. And if he had just left you alone, you'd have been fine. I always knew you loved me. I always knew that, Jordan. Because you wear your love all over your face. And I stuck around anyway."

"Why?" I ask.

He shrugs. "That's what friends do."

I just stare at him. And now my eyes are glassy. "I'm fucked up, Ix. I'm really fucked up. That girl, that night, here… she called it playing games. She played a game with me. And somehow I took that and made it who I was. Somehow—"

But Ixion has crossed the small space that separates us. He sits down on the couch next to me, puts his arm around my neck, and pulls me in to a hug.

Not a bro hug. A real hug.

"Somehow," I continue, "I took her game and made it mine."

"So what?" he says, still hugging me. "So what?"

I pull back, wiping my eyes. "So I fuck with people. The way she fucked with me. I scare them, and make them uncomfortable, and I like it. Because she did that to me and I hated it. I want to be her, the one in control, and not me, the scared kid. I want to hurt people, Ixion."

"You're stupid," he says. "Who have you hurt?"

"You," I say. "Augustine. Alexander. I ruined everything because I played these stupid games. I ruined all of us."

"Come on," he says. "You're not that important. You're not that powerful. You can't take credit for my fuckups. Those are all mine, asshole. And you're certainly not gonna take credit for my happiness, either. Also all mine."

"You took the blame for me," I say. "Why did you do that? And don't say that's what friends do. No one takes that kind of blame to save a friend. Not when said friend fucked you over."

He smiles. Shakes his head a little. Then frowns. "Because you always had a future, and I never did."

"You're a goddamned billionaire, Ixion. Your family had more money than God. You did have a future before I fucked it up. And now look at you! You're—"

"I'm fucking perfect."

"Your whole family is dead!" I say. "That's what Evangeline and I are hiding from you! That house I live in? That beautiful empty mansion that used to hold a family? Well, they all died last year in a car crash. That's why I'm here. It made me realize what I took from you—"

"Stop being an asshole," Ixion barks. "They died in a car crash. A drunk driver killed them."

"But they all died thinking you made that sex tape. They all died thinking you were a criminal. And you were sitting in jail and didn't even get to go to the funeral. They all died thinking—"

"They died thinking of me the way they saw me, Jordan. My father never said, 'Tell me what happened, Ix. I'm on your side. I'll believe you if you say you're innocent. I'll help you if you say you're not.' He never said that. He said…" Ixion pauses.

"He said what?" I ask.

Ix swallows hard and takes a deep breath. "He said… 'I always knew you'd end up this way.' And yeah, maybe your dad's an asshole. No, he *is* an asshole. But at least… at least he always had your back. My dad never had my back. My dad accused me of stealing his good cognac, and fucking things up with his mistress, and—"

"That was me!" I say.

"I know, dumbass!" And then he laughs. "I know it was you! He probably knew it was you too! But he wanted it to be me. He *wanted* it to be *me*, Jordan."

There's a long silence in the room. I think we're both holding our breath.

"He wanted it to be me, so it was. He hated me and that's all there is to it. He said he was cutting me out of the will. And if they had died a few days later, he would've and I'd have been left penniless. But they didn't, they died that day. And I had nothing to do with it. And you had nothing to do with it. And fuck it, right? I miss my little sister. She didn't deserve that. But… but I refuse to feel guilty because they died and I lived. I did that already. I spent eight years doing that. And then you know what happened? One day Jordan Wells pulls me out of a jail cell, cashes in a favor he didn't want to use, and gives me a second chance at happiness. So fuck off with your bullshit guilt, Wells. OK? Just fuck off. Because what I'm really here to say is…"

He reaches for my shoulder. Grips it with his hand and I'm holding my breath again.

"Is thank you, man. Just… thank you. Things go the way they go and what comes out the other end is exactly what you put into it. That's all there is to life. What you get is what you give. And you give a whole hell of a lot, Jordan. A whole helluva lot."

He stares at me. Waiting for my reaction. His eyes almost pleading with me to say something.

I breathe. Internalize. And then say, "You wanna kiss me, don't you?"

He pushes me away, laughing. "Fuck you."

But then… but then he reaches for me again. And he does.

He kisses me. It's a nice kiss too. Right on the lips. No tongue or anything like that. No passion or romance. It's just innocent, and nice, and perfect.

And when he pulls back he says, "That's all I got for you."

And I say, "It's more than I deserve."

CHAPTER FOURTEEN

We take separate cars back to Denver because—obviously. And he goes his way and I go my way, except… I don't know where to go.

I don't want to go home. I don't want to think about that house. But I don't want to go to the Bartos house either. I could go to work, but the day is pretty much over and my father might be there.

I do not want to see him right now. I have not even begun to sort through those feelings yet.

So I go to the only place I can go.

Chella's.

Is it weird that my new best friend is a married woman?

"What the fuck?" Smith says when he opens their front door. "Dude, why are you always dropping by?"

Obviously her husband thinks it is.

"Because she's on maternity leave and I can't just pop over to her tea room."

"Is that Jordan?" Chella calls from somewhere inside the house. "Yay! Company!"

I give Smith a smug smile and push past him and make my way into the living room at the back of the house.

"Hey!" Chella says.

"Hey," I say back, leaning down to kiss her cheek. "Wow, look at this guy! He's adorable."

She sighs as she holds her sleeping newborn son in her arms. "I know. He's so perfect. Such a good sleeper already."

Smith grunts and takes a seat in the chair across from the couch.

"What?" Chella says. "Four hours at a time—that's like a miracle, Smith. And he's not bothered at all by the dogs when they bark. He's already an animal lover. He's so… easy-going."

"So you say," Smith says. Clearly new fatherhood is taking its toll on him because his eyes are bloodshot and he's got the beginnings of dark circles underneath.

"Hmm. He must take after you, Chella."

Smith shoots me a look. "So what is it now, Wells? What problem do you have that only my wife can solve?"

"If it's a bad time—"

"It's not," Chella insists, standing up and walking over to a bassinet and laying the baby down. He fusses and coos for a moment and Chella shushes him as she pats his back. "No one is coming by to visit me. I feel like a shut-in."

I glance at Smith and he looks appropriately guilty. He's been keeping people away.

"No one but this guy."

"I never got the memo," I say, kinda glad I dropped by. And not just because it drives Smith crazy, either. But because they're so normal now. It gives me hope. Like… maybe I have a future. Maybe I'm not hopeless.

I mean, they were me when they met. Maybe even worse than me. They were some pretty fucked-up people a couple years ago. Smith and his weird quirks. Chella desperate to get over her past.

Separate they were lost, but together… together they are a spectacular team.

"You ever worry..." But I stop. Because I shouldn't bring my bullshit in here. They're so happy. And it was a tough road for them. It wasn't easy but they pulled it off.

"Do we ever worry what?" Chella asks.

"Never mind."

"No, say it," Smith says. "Do we ever worry about what?"

I run my fingers through my hair. "Do ya ever worry you'll fuck him up?" They both just stare at me. "Forget it," I say hurriedly. "Never mind. Of course not, you guys are—"

"A fuckin' mess?" Chella says. She smiles at me. "Because we are? Because we're human and we make mistakes. And we all have this baggage we carry around. And then yeah, you get pregnant and all those fuck-ups your parents made suddenly come rushing back."

"And you ask yourself," Smith says, picking it up. "'Will I do the same? Will I fail him?'"

I nod. "Yeah. All that."

"I think if we didn't have that fear," Smith says, "I'd be *more* worried about us."

I nod again. "You guys are gonna kill this parenting stuff. I can tell."

"You will too, Jordan," Chella says. "One day, when you find the right people"—and I laugh at that. Because she knows me. And she loves me anyway—"you guys are gonna rock the family shit. You're one of the good ones."

"Fuck," I say. But my throat is tight and my eyes are watering. "No, I'm not. What I do, what I did—"

"What you did," Chella says, interrupting me, "for me... that was a gift. OK?"

And I don't know what she's talking about. Killing her father? Or just being her friend?

I look to Smith for help and he gives me a weak smile. "She knows it was you. And I told her I paid you."

"He also told me you didn't cash the check yet."

I shake my head. "No. I can't take that money. I shouldn't have played that game. I shouldn't have played any of them. It's all fucked up, you guys."

"What is?" Chella says.

"Me," I say. "I'm so fucked up." I lean forward, elbows on knees, staring down at my shoes. A position of defeat I'm starting to get used to.

"Is this about Augustine and Alexander? Did something happen?"

I shake my head, unable to look her in the face. "No, it's not about them."

"Then who?" Smith asks. "I'm fuckin' buffed out these days, dude. Fighting those damn teenagers down at the gym has got me ripped. I can mess people up for you."

I can't help it, I laugh and look up at him.

"No shit, man. You need some muscle? I'm down."

"I don't need muscle, dumbass. I have Darrel and Finn, remember?"

He reaches out, fist first, and I lean forward and give him a bump.

"Then who?" Chella asks.

And then I have to make a decision. To pull out all my neatly-folded secrets or keep them packed up in that fucking suitcase I'm carrying around.

And I don't know what it is about Chella that makes me want to confess things to her. What makes me want to hear her opinions and ask her advice. But I do.

So I start from the beginning. Not that night when I was twelve, that wasn't the beginning. I start with the day the Club closed. How I drank myself unconscious. And then the games that came after. And Ixion, and all those messy feelings that come with him. And the house and why I can't go home.

It ends with the night at the cabin when I was twelve and then I let out a long breath and wait for their judgment.

"Wow," Chella says.

I look at Smith. He says, "Fuck... that... asshole." And then he stands up and paces the floor. "Just fuck him. You know what, Jordan?"

"What?" I say, taken aback at his sudden anger.

He points his finger at me. "You don't owe him shit, OK? You don't *owe him shit*. You don't owe him an explanation about who you are or what kind of people you want to share your intimate moments with. You don't owe him a goddamned success story or... or... a fucking law career. Or even a fucking promise to do your best. Because his job was pretty simple. Be. Your. Father. That's it. And you need to tell him that."

"You think?"

"Smith," Chella says, interrupting. "I mean, he should do what he wants. Don't tell him that."

"No," Smith says, shaking his head. Still pacing the floor back and forth in front of the kitchen island. "No. I did that, Jordan. I didn't confront them. And I don't know Ixion but I know his story. He didn't confront his father either. But you know what?" And now he's looking at Chella.

"What?" she says, pouting her lips.

"We confronted your father." He says it in a very low, even tone. Smith pivots his head to look at me now. "And that asshole didn't have a regretful bone in his body. Fuck him. Fuck all of them. Why are people so uptight about this shit? I mean, good God, dude. He was afraid you were gay so he bought you sex at twelve? How does that even make sense?"

"I dunno," I whisper. "It doesn't. I think that's why it bothers me so much. Like… what was he thinking? How could he be so… I dunno. Careless with me?"

"No," Chella says. "No, it bothers you because it was wrong. It bothers you because he's supposed to love you unconditionally. It bothers you because he was your father and in his eyes, you were less than perfect. And I know I'm going to make mistakes with Daniel. We both are. But we will never make him feel bad about being himself. Ever."

Smith just looks at her. He looks at her like she's a goddess. Like she's an endless fountain of wisdom and strength. Like there is no love greater than this love he feels for his wife. And then he gives her one of this infamous Smith smiles and nods. "Ever," he echoes.

I end up staying the night in one of the second-floor guest rooms. And in the morning Smith hands me a suit from his closet and says, "Gotta run. But we're pretty close to the same size, so have a suit on me. Coffee's in the kitchen, Chella's sleeping, and if you need to sleep here tonight too, just… you know." He shrugs. "Show up. You're always welcome here."

"Thanks," I say.

"Hey, I once spent years bouncing around from friend to friend, making them support me because I refused to own anything, that's how afraid I was of turning into my father. I get you," he says, pointing at me. "We get you.

And we got you, too. You need someone to kill your old man?"

I laugh, I can't help it.

"I'm your guy, Jordan. Just say the word."

"Thanks," I say, grabbing the suit. "I needed to hear that. But," I add quickly, just in case he's serious, "I'm gonna pass on the offer."

He shoots me with his finger. "Offer stands. Forever."

It occurs to me, as I drive into work, that I have a lot of pretty cool friends.

CHAPTER FIFTEEN

I want to avoid my father today, but of course there he is standing at the reception desk talking to Gail, who outs me with a cheery, "Hope you're feeling better today, Jordan."

My father turns and smiles. Because he has no clue what's inside me. None. I mean, why should he? It's been more than fifteen years since that night at the cabin. If it ever bothered him, that passed. Long ago. "Sorry to hear you were sick, Jordan. Why didn't you call your mother? She'd have brought you some chicken soup. You know how good it is." He chuckles, squeezing my arm as we walk into the private reception area and head down the hallway to our offices.

"It wasn't that kind of sick, Dad. I just needed a break, that's all."

"Oh. Things come up in your little"—he cups his hand to his mouth and whispers—"game?"

"No, Dad. No. I was just overworked, I think. I just needed some time." And this is something I don't get either. The fact that he kinda knows what I do on the side. I mean, he doesn't have details or anything, and he certainly doesn't know anything about killing Chella's father or taking down a couple of corrupt FBI agents, but he knows I run this little fantasy game.

He claps me on the back and says, "I'm back with you. So where have your friends been, Jordan?"

For a second I think he's referring to Augustine and Alexander. But then I realize he's talking about Finn and Darrel. "They're not friends, Dad. They're business associates. And we're…" I shrug. "Not very busy at the moment, so I dunno where they are. Doing whatever they do."

"Good," he says. "Good. Is there a new girl in your life?"

I stop in the hallway just outside my office. "Why are you asking me all these questions?" It comes out haughty. Because I am. Being haughty, that is.

"You caught me." He laughs.

"Caught you doing what?"

"Your mother. She's been after me to get you over for dinner because she wants to set you up with the daughter of one of her friends."

"No," I say. My mother pulls this at least twice a year. Most of the time I successfully avoid the painful blind date, but every once in a while, she sneaks one in on me and then pretends she didn't have anything to do with it.

"I told her you wouldn't be receptive. But she wants to ask you herself. So I told her you'd come over for dinner tonight. Be there at seven."

"Whoa, whoa, whoa," I say, reaching out to grab his arm. "I'm not coming."

"Oh, tonight is not the date. There's no surprise girl jumping our from under the dining room table, I promise you. Now I gotta go. First day back after the tests—"

"Hey, how did that go?"

"I'm fine," he says, his smile wide as it ever was. "Just fine. See you tonight."

With that he walks off.

I shut my office door, sit down at my desk, and pull up my calendar.

Blank.

I push the button on my phone for Eileen. "Yes, Jordan?"

"Why is my calendar empty?"

"Oh, your father said to clear it. Said you needed a day off."

"What did I have on there? Did I have court?"

"No, no," Eileen replies. "It was just some paperwork today. I have your paralegal on it. No need to worry."

I slump back in my chair. "Thanks."

I think.

Like what is going on with my father?

My phone buzzes in my coat pocket, so I take it out and look at the screen. Augustine.

For a moment I hesitate. Because I don't really want to talk to them. I don't think this is working. I mean, I like them. It's fun and it feels good, but… seriously, where do I think this is going?

And for that matter, where am I going?

I let Augustine go to voicemail and instead press the contact for my real-estate agent, Lawton Ayers.

"Hey," he says, unceremoniously. "I was just thinking about you."

"Yeah, why's that?"

"That house you have? The mansion everyone's so keen to know more about these days?"

"What about it?"

"I have a buyer."

"It's not for sale. Unless it's Ixion. Is it Ixion?"

"No, it's a corporation."

"What corporation?"

"Something called…" There's a shuffling of papers on the other end of the phone. "Standard License LLC."

"So a shell corporation?"

"Looks like it."

"Why is everyone so interested in this house?"

"I was gonna ask you the same thing. I mean, it's a cool house, no doubt. But it was on the market for over a month last year before you bought it. So why now? Why didn't they swoop in when they could get it at foreclosure pricing?"

"I have no clue," I say absently. Weird.

"So what'd you want?"

"Oh, well. Ironically, I was calling about the house. So… Evangeline told me what happened to that family."

"Yeah, that sucks, right? So sad."

"Yeah. Sad."

"Uh… and?" Law says. "What about it?"

"I dunno. It's just weird."

"I can't say I disagree, but… I can't say why I feel that way, either."

"Find out who owns that shell, can you do that?"

"Probably not." He laughs. "I mean, they have a shell for a reason, right? Better get one of your guys on that if you need that kind of digging." And then he pauses. "Everything OK with you?"

"Yup," I say. "Thanks." And then I end the call.

But something is not OK. I just can't figure out what it is.

Everything seems just a little out of whack. Like the world has tilted. Shifted while I wasn't looking.

Augustine and Alexander came back this year. Right after that game I set up with Evangeline and Ixion.

So really… Augustine and Alexander came back at the *same time* as Ixion.

Yeah. Didn't really put those two things together before now. I was avoiding Augustine last winter. Didn't want anything to do with her. With them.

But how did they get here? I mean, I get it. Sort of. They were having trouble, they said. Thought I was their answer.

But why now? After all these years? Because they were having trouble long before now. They separated years ago. Got back together years ago. So what's been going on between then and now? That's something they never shared with me.

I call Law back and when he picks up and says, "What now?" I say, "Get that contract ready for the sale of the old Turning Point. I'm buying it in about…" I check my calendar to see when my three-week deal with Augustine is up. "Ten days."

Law laughs. "Uh… well. I don't know what to say to that."

"What do you mean?"

"Well, it's not for sale."

"Yeah, but you said Augustine and Alexander own the shell. And we've got a deal in place. So in ten days they're selling it to me. No questions asked."

"OK," Law says, still hesitating. "Do they have an agent?"

"Shit. I dunno. Just be prepared. I want that deal done the second I'm eligible. I've got cash saved so it should go quick."

"What are you gonna do with it?"

"Open it back up." I laugh. "What the fuck else would I do with it?"

We say goodbye and hang up and then I just sit there for a second.

Because… am I going to open it back up?

Suddenly I'm not so sure.

So I just sit there in my office thinking. Nothing to do today except think.

I go back eight months to the house. Because for some reason everything goes back to that house.

I call Evangeline.

"Hey, Jordan, what's up?" She sounds out of breath, like she's been running.

"Am I interrupting something?" I ask.

"No, not really. I'm walking the treadmill as I play the violin. It's a training exercise. I have a show planned for late fall and I'm trying to step up my game and… you know, do something kinda flashy. I'm tired of classical music and why should I have to sit down or stand still while I play? You ever see fiddlers, Jordan?"

"Fiddlers?" I ask, suddenly lost.

"Yeah, you know how they go crazy on stage and do these little dances and shit? I think I want to be a fiddler. I'm putting the band back together."

Which makes me huff out a laugh. I thought Evangeline was kinda stuffy and uptight when I first met her. But I was wrong. She's kinda… funny. And weird. But in a cool way.

"What band?" I ask. Because I can't *not* ask.

"That was a joke. I don't have a band. But I'm gonna get one. I'm having auditions and I'm gonna put together a fiddler band. You know anyone who plays the banjo?"

This time I don't hold in the laugh. It comes out like a guffaw. "Oh, my God. You just made my day. But no, I don't know any banjo players."

"I know," she says. And I can almost hear her smile. "I just wanted to throw you off balance today and make you happy because Ixion came home last night and... wow. Whatever you guys did, it made him happy. I wanted to make you happy back. So what'd you need?"

"You know my house?"

"Yeah?"

"You never told me their name. Who was that family?"

I write down the name, tell her good luck with the fiddler band, and hang up.

A few seconds later, my phone buzzes. It's Augustine again.

But I let her go to voicemail as I walk out of my office and tell everyone I'll be back tomorrow.

Because I'm dialing Darrel's number.

At six forty-five I'm sitting in my car down the street from my parents' home, waiting for Darrel's call. I feel sick. Like... wanna-throw-up sick. I don't know why. It's just that feeling you get in your gut when someone unleashes a secret you didn't see coming. Some terrible thing, only it didn't just happen. It's been happening for a long time and you never knew about it.

A girl cheated on me once. I was in college at Stanford and I was like, I dunno. Nineteen. And we'd been going out for a while. Like all through freshman year and into sophomore year. A pretty long time for college. And I really thought I loved this girl. Like couldn't eat kinda love, ya know? The kind that just stops your life and you feel like you can't go on without them. Can't work, or pay attention to anything. Can't imagine living without them. Or you can, it just looks like misery.

And she'd dodge my calls. Not show up for dates. Shit like that. And I'd ask her, "Are you seeing someone else? Do you wanna break up?" Because that's how I deal with conflict. I just want the truth.

And she'd always say, "No, of course not. I love you."

And that was all I wanted to hear. All I needed to hear. OK, she loves me. And she'd stick around for a week or two and everything would be great.

But it always happened again.

She'd just ghost me. Just disappear and forget about me.

And then I wound up in this downward spiral of depression. I lived in this stupid apartment off-campus in sophomore year and I can remember so clearly sitting in bed listening for the sound of her shoes on the metal stairs outside that led up to the apartment.

Like… I *knew* that sound. I knew it. And every time someone else would come up the stairs, like a neighbor, I'd hope it was her, but I knew it wasn't.

And it wasn't.

I almost failed two classes that fall semester. That's how off my game she had me. And looking back, God, why? Why did I act that way? I don't miss her. So that love wasn't real.

But she consumed me. She ate me up from the inside out.

Because I knew she was cheating. I knew it. I just let her lie to me because it made me feel better. Made the food go down. Made me able to study for a few hours. Made the day pass.

And after she ghosted she'd always come back. Why? Like just why did she come back?

That's the part that fucked me up so badly.

Because the truth is she was using me. It was a plan. It was plotted. She needed me. For money, for a place to live every time she couldn't pay her rent and asked to crash at my place. And I'd be like, "Just move in. Then you don't have to worry about it. Just move in and be with me. Use my car, here, take my credit card and buy whatever you need."

And she stayed that last time. Said OK and took everything I offered her.

But she didn't stop. And she didn't start loving me either.

Instead of me calling her obsessively, or driving by her apartment to see if she was there with someone else, or asking my friends if they'd seen her, I just… I just stayed home in bed, listening for her footsteps on the stairs.

Waiting for her key in the lock.

Hoping she'd come back because somehow she'd made it so I couldn't live without her.

How do people do that?

It's weird.

She disappeared for good after that.

And then one day at the end of senior year I saw her with this guy at a park just a few blocks off campus. And there was a kid there. A little baby, like… I dunno. Less than a year, for sure. They were taking turns pushing him in one of those baby swings and he was laughing, and smiling, and having a good time.

So I got out of my car and walked up towards the playground. And she saw me, and then he saw me, and she picked the baby up and turned her back, and he headed straight at me, hand out in front of him. One of those *stay back* gestures.

And he said, "He's not yours. So don't start no shit. We did the DNA test a long time ago, Jordan. Just leave her alone."

And it hit me.

That feeling in my gut.

When I realized that he knew me. He knew all about me. And it didn't even matter if it was lies. Because of course, *whatever he thought he knew*, it was all lies.

I just felt violated because he *knew* me.

And I knew nothing about him.

Because he was the real boyfriend and I was the other man.

I just never knew it.

Even though I don't think about her, I do think about him. I wonder… did he ever figure out who she really was? Did he ever figure out that everything she told him was a lie?

And I feel really sad for him. For that kid, too.

Because people who lie like that… it's a psychosis. It's a mental illness.

And people like him… like me… we just live with it.

Because it makes the food go down.

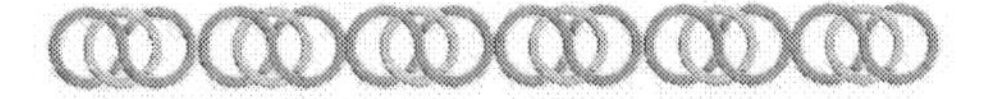

My phone buzzes on the seat next to me, drawing me out of the past. I reach over, pick it up, and accept Darrel's call.

"Give me something," I say.

"Shit, I had to pull favors for this one. Someone really wanted these people to stay unknown."

"What? Why? Why do you say that?"

"Because, OK, look. I got their names. Nathan and Marie Thompson."

"OK?"

"And the kids are Chris, he's the teen boy. Then Rylee, the small girl. And Abbey, the baby."

"Right."

"But it's Marie Thompson I had trouble with."

And this is when that feeling comes back. "Why?" I ask.

"Because I couldn't find her real name. Like, she changed her maiden name before she got married. But I had a hunch her new maiden name was her old middle name, because it was Sara. Marie Sara. So I went digging for Marie Sara's old name. And bingo. Got her."

"Who is she?"

"A very troubled girl, from what I can tell. Sealed juvenile records. Like sealed up motherfucking tight, ya know?"

"Shit," I say.

"But I got a judge to open them," he says. "And I got a picture. Sending it now."

I stare at my phone, waiting for the ding of a message.

I know what she looks like. At thirty-five, anyway. Because I saw the pictures before I dropped them off at Law's office weeks ago.

But what I really need to know now is… what did she look like at seventeen?

"There he is!" my father says as I walk through their front door. I can smell dinner. Smells of my childhood.

Roast chicken, and potatoes, and a hint of spicy seasoning that's probably my mother's homemade salad dressing.

He claps me on the back and says, "Did you have a nice day off?"

"Well," I say, walking into the large open kitchen area where my mom is cooking. She turns and looks over her shoulder at me, smiling as she wipes her hands on her apron.

My mother is classic upper class. By that I mean the old-school kind. Not modern-day I-can-have-my-cake-and-eat-it-too. Not at all. Janet Wells made a choice back when she was twenty-two, and that choice was to be wife to Jack Wells and mother to yet-to-be Jordan Wells. That was her choice, and even though I'd often look at Ixion's mother and think, *God, she's different*—always going places, always involved in things, always… missing when it came to Ixion, which is why his house was the perfect place to hang when we were smaller—I used to think, *That's not my mother*. She doesn't look like my mother in any way.

My mother is Barbara Bush classy. She wears tailored suits and dresses. Pearls and subdued makeup.

Ixion's mom… let's call her Melania. She was flashy. Maybe a little bit slutty, if I'm being honest. Not that she wasn't a lovely lady. She was. Just not the same kind of lovely as my mom.

Ixion's parents were always loud. They argued like it was a sport. Like the winner got prize money at the end. It was a lot of swearing, and arm-flailing, and dramatic accusations.

My parents… I don't think I've ever heard my parents argue.

"It's so nice to see you, Jordan," my mom says, placing both hands on my cheeks and giving me a kiss. "What have you been up to?"

"What have I been up to?" I mumble, looking at my father. He's got his back to me, grabbing us drinks from the bar.

"What's that?" my mom asks.

I look down at the folder in my hand and wonder…

"Here," my father says. "Come sit down and have a drink while your mother finishes with dinner. Leave the boy alone, Janet. He's working hard, that's what he's been up to."

I'm looking at my mother when he says that, her smile falling a little further with each word. But then she rallies and the smile is back. "Go have your drink. Dinner is almost ready." She rubs my arm and then the smile is real. Just for a moment, it's real.

She turns and goes back to her meal prep.

So I take my attention to my father, who is already sitting in his oversized wingback leather chair, sipping his Scotch.

"What is that?" my father says, nodding his head to my folder.

I toss it down on the coffee table in front of the couch, then pick up my drink from a coaster and take a seat in the matching wingback chair that faces his. "There's something I need to ask you," I say, looking down into the glass of dark amber liquid. I consider taking a drink, but then decide not to, and set it back down on the little side table to my left.

"Shoot," my father says. "What's on your mind, Jordan?"

I glance at my mother, who is all the way across the large room, still busy doing something with dinner, not paying any attention to us, and then take my full attention back to my father. "How long?" I ask.

He smiles at me. "What? How long what?"

I glance at my mother again, making sure she's not listening. "How long did you keep Marie Sara Claiborne as one of your little sex slaves?"

His eyes narrow as he calmly tracks them to the kitchen. To my mother. To make sure she's not listening. "Keep your fucking voice down," he whispers.

"When did you get her?" I ask. "How old was she? Because when you sent her to me that night in the cabin, she was definitely not eighteen."

"We can talk about this later, after—"

"Fuck that," I say. My voice is low. Even. But very clearly angry. "Fuck. That. We're talking abut it now. Did you kill her? Did you kill that family last year?"

"What fucking family?" my father growls.

"The Thompsons. Because Marie Sara Claiborne turned into Marie Sara Thompson. Funny how you never mentioned that I bought the house they used to live in. Seeing as how…" And I have to stop here. Because this… this was the hardest thing to hear. Of all the revelations Darrel told me on the phone ten minutes ago, this was the hardest. But it needs to be said. "Seeing as how her oldest child was my half-brother."

That poor fucking kid. He looked like such a good kid. Such a normal fucking kid.

And it kills me now. Knowing I had a chance to… I don't know, look through his room? Find clues about who he was? And I just threw it all away and sold the rest off in an estate sale.

I sold my only sibling off in an estate sale.

My father glances at my mother again. She's in the kitchen humming. And I'm not sure if that's just something she does these days, or if she's deliberately trying to drown out the conversation going on in her living room. "It was an accident."

"Fuck you it was an accident. Was bringing Marie up to see me when I was twelve an accident? Was telling her to fix me an accident too?"

"You're getting this all wrong. I'm trying to help you, Jordan."

"Help me do what?" I ask.

"Help you navigate your way through the… through the personality issues you have, son."

I actually laugh. "Personality issues? Is that what you're calling it? No," I say, shaking my head. "We're not gonna talk in code tonight. It's called bisexual, Dad. I'm bisexual."

He puts his hand up and says, "Just wait a minute. That's not what it was about."

"No? Funny. Marie Sara told me that's exactly what it was about. I'm supposed to like girls, right? Well, newsflash, I do like girls. I just like them with guys."

"I'm not judging you, Jordan. I just wanted to make things easier for you than they were for me. What's wrong with that?"

And that's when all the shit Darrel just told me slides into place. That folder is thick with evidence he's collected. My father's past. His history.

And it looks uncomfortably similar to mine.

"I didn't judge you when you got involved with those people in LA. I didn't judge you when you joined that club.

I didn't judge you when you started up this game business. And do you know why I didn't judge you, Jordan?"

I swallow. Because I do. Only I don't want to hear it.

"That's right," he says. "I had those relationships too. I had clubs like that too. I played my own games back in my day."

"You killed her," I say, hurling the accusation with absolute calm. "You killed her, and you killed her family, and then… then what? Did you somehow convince me to buy that house? Is there evidence there? Was that…" Oh, shit. I want to throw up. "Was that house your… club?"

He glances at my mother again. And now I'm sure she knows we're in here discussing things. I'm sure she's hiding in her kitchen. I'm sure she's pretending she can't hear this conversation.

Because she's been doing it her whole adult life. Pretending that Jack Wells was a pretty good catch.

I don't need an answer. Because I already know. In the three seconds since those words came out of my mouth everything fell into place.

My father had a sex club. Only it wasn't husbands and wives looking to swing or add a third or fourth. It wasn't consensual. It was… something *sick*. Something poisonous. Something that led to Marie Sara being driven up to the Washakie Ten cabin to service a twelve-year-old when she was only a kid herself.

It was games, all right. It was dark secrets, and dark places, and my mother. Here, in this house, pretending it wasn't happening.

I just stand up and say, "Mom. I can't stay. I just got a call and I…I have to take it. It's an emergency. But I'll… I'll come by next weekend or something, I promise."

"Jordan!" she calls after me.

But my father cuts her off with a sharp, "Go back in the kitchen, Janet," and follows me to the front door.

I swing it open, letting it bang hard against the doorstop, and just hop down the front steps towards my car.

"It's not what you think," my father says. "And frankly, some of what you're saying sounds insane. Just ludicrous."

"Is it?" I say, halting my escape so I can turn to face him one last time. "Then tell me what I'm missing."

He shakes his head a few times. Standing there, looking down at me from just across the threshold of the doorway, trying to find the words.

He's never going to find them.

There are no words that can excuse what he is.

"I didn't have anything to do with you buying that house. I have no idea what possessed you to purchase it." He stops to stare at me. And for a second I see the dad I thought I knew. The one who taught me how to play t-ball with me in the back yard. The one who showed up for parent-teacher conferences in second grade. The one who took me turkey hunting the fall I turned ten.

"Where did you go?" I ask him. "What happened to you? How could you do this? To me? To them? How?"

"I… I don't know what you're talking about. Just… Jordan, listen to me. Just… just let it go. Dragging things up from the past rarely fixes things. I know that better than most. But I was desperate, that's all. I'm sorry. Just move on and forget about them. You got along just fine before they came back. You can do it again. Just—"

"Wait, what? What did you just say?"

"I said you got along just fine. You were doing just fine. I'm sorry. I should've left well enough alone. I see that now. I just… I didn't want you to buy that building."

"What?"

"You need to let that place go, Jordan. Just like I did when my partners and I sold it."

"*What*? You and your—"

Holy fucking shit.

I did have it wrong. My father wasn't running a sex club in the mansion.

He was one of the original owners of Turning Point.

I just shake my head at him. "I feel sorry for you." And then movement over his shoulder catches my attention… and there's my mother, standing in the hallway, wiping her hands on her apron. Her eyes lock onto mine and she frowns.

My father follows my line of sight, turns, and snaps, "Go *back to the kitchen*, Janet!"

She turns away without a word and then he's talking again.

"I had to keep them away from you. All of them. Your… your entire future was at stake, Jordan. You knew that as well as I did. That's why you blamed Ixion."

At the mention of Ix's name I freeze. I lose time. I… I don't know what happens to me, other than that sick feeling in my gut turns into something even more revolting.

"You," I say, looking up at my father and meeting his gaze.

"I did what I had to. Just like you did."

"No," I say, shaking my head. "No…"

"I need you to take over the firm, Jordan. Do you think that my partners will continue my legacy? Do you think I built this empire just to let it fade with my death? No," he says. "No. You were born for a reason, son. And now it's time to take your place."

"What the *fuck* are you talking about?"

"He was going to turn you in. You would've been kicked out of law school. Banned from practicing even before you got your degree. What you did was a felony, Jordan. That's why you blamed him in the first place. You knew he'd be confused and take the fall. Because you two were tight. You practically groomed him from childhood to be your fall guy. And I know you think you loved him, hell, maybe you think he loved you back. I don't know. But this was not a forever kind of deal. This was a heat-of-the-moment deal. You *knew* he would sell you out. The minute he got word that his father disowned him and wrote him out of the will, he would've sold. You. Out."

"No," I whisper, shaking my head. "No. Never."

I don't even feel the need to fight about it.

It just is.

Never would Ixion *ever* do to me what I did to him.

So I turn, and walk away, and don't look back.

Because my father isn't worth the breath it would take to explain how I know that.

CHAPTER SIXTEEN

I don't know how I feel about this… this… strange multi-generational story that I have unwittingly become a part of. The circle of deceit, and lust, and game-playing rocks me back on my heels and begs for a solution.

But what kind of solution?

The most disturbing thing of this whole day might be that I can't think straight. Can't make sense of any of it.

I am the one who always has the answer. *I* am the game master. *I* am the one who controls all the pieces on the chessboard. *I* am the one who determines the winners and losers.

And now I find out all these years I've been nothing but a player in his sick game.

I don't even know what that game is. I don't want to know what that game is.

I just want out.

My phone rings and when I look at the screen it's Alexander.

I don't answer it, not because I don't want to. I do. I want to tell them everything. I want to tell everyone everything.

But I'm driving and… I just don't know how to start that conversation. Because I don't even know what I'm into.

I have no fucking clue.

So I drive over to their house, park on the crowded street a few blocks down, and walk to their building by way of the park, texting him back to let him know I'm on my way.

When I get up to their floor, the double doors to the penthouse are already open. Augustine is standing there, backlit by the setting sun, frowning.

"Fuck," I say, running my hands through my hair.

"Where have you been? We've been looking for you for two days!"

"Out," I say.

"You haven't been home," she says, taking my arm and pulling me inside.

"No," I say.

Because that mansion isn't my home. That mansion was Marie Sara's home. Her and her husband, Chad Thompson. And her teen boy, my half-brother, Chris. And her little girl, Rylee.

And little baby Abbey.

And now, because of my father, they are all dead.

And for some sick, sick reason… I bought that house and now I live in it.

Why the fuck did I buy that house?

How did I even hear about it? Law? Someone else?

No… no, it was an email. It was just a stupid LuxuryHouseHunt.com email. *We have a home you might be interested in…*

"Jordan!" Augustine snaps.

"What?" I say, snapping out of my introspection.

"Are you even hearing me? Come inside."

I do, I follow her inside and focus on Alexander, standing in front of the window that overlooks the park and the downtown skyline.

"You have to let us explain," he says, just as I hear the definitive click of the doors closing.

"Dude, I don't even know where to start with this shit. I mean…"

"It wasn't our fault," Augustine says. "We had to."

"Wait. What?" And that's when the feeling comes back. That heavy stone in the pit of my stomach.

"We *were* going to get that building for you," Alexander says. "It was just gonna take some time. And that's why we needed the three weeks, OK? It isn't what it looks like, I swear, it isn't." His words are spilling out too fast as he paces back and forth across the living room space.

"We were just playing along, Jordan," Augustine says. "We were… we had a plan. And I know it looks bad now, but if you let us explain, you'll see we had no choice. We had to."

"What. The fuck. Are you talking about?"

But I already know. Have known this whole time, haven't I?

They came looking for me only after I brought Ixion home.

"No," I say, shaking my head at them. "No."

But it's a just a reflex to help me process. Or wishful thinking. Or one last attempt to make the food go down and pretend none of this is happening.

"You don't own that building, do you?"

"You have to let us explain," Augustine says.

"DO YOU OWN THAT BUILDING?" I scream it.

"He made us, Jordan. You don't understand. He made us play along and—"

"He made you… he *made you*… fuck me? Is that what you're telling me?"

"Listen," Alexander says.

"No, you fucking listen! Who owns that building?"

Augustine just shakes her head.

"My father, he owns it, doesn't he? You were never going to sell it to me, were you? This whole thing is just another part of his sick game. Did he pay you? Did you sit up at night, all those months while I was ignoring you, and plot how to make me believe you… you… fucking loved me?"

"Jordan," Augustine says. "You *have* to let us explain. We—"

"Fuck you," I say. "Just fuck you both."

I have no house. I can't go back to that house.

I have no job. I won't go back to that job.

I have no family. Probably never did. I was just a pawn in some sick game I don't even understand and never want to.

I never want to know what they were planning for me.

Ever.

So I go to the only person I have left.

Ixion opens the door to the penthouse he shares with Evangeline overlooking the 16th Street Mall, frowning.

"Dude," he says.

But I just step forward into the apartment, unable to meet Evangeline's obviously concerned gaze, and stop in front of the window. Press my hands and forehead against the glass, and say, "Who the fuck am I?"

Because I don't know anymore.

I tell them the whole story. I don't leave a single thing out. I don't keep a single secret locked up inside me.

I tell. The whole. Story.

At some point I realize I left that folder of evidence on the coffee table in my parents' living room. But it doesn't matter. It was just copies Darrel gave me.

And when I'm done talking I turn around and face them. "I quit," I say. "I quit. Because a very smart woman once told me sometimes the only way to win the game is to quit the game. So I just… quit."

I walk over to their couch, slump down against the cushions, and just stare at the ceiling as they talk, or ask me questions, or whatever.

Because I check out.

The one person you never want on your side is the person who can't accept themselves for who they are. The one who was like you, but pretends he isn't.

It's the smoker who quit and then berates everyone else about smoking.

It's the newly converted vegan who turns their nose up at your burger.

It's the alcoholic who thinks they have it under control, but you don't.

The one person you never want on your side is the hypocrite.

And the hypocrite is me.

At some point, Chella and Smith show up. And Chella sits on the couch next to me and just folds me into her arms. She just hugs me.

I don't even know how long we stay like that, but eventually she's leading me down to her car in the closest parking garage, and then we're at her house down on Little

Raven Street. And I'm walked up to their second-floor guest room and put to bed.

I think I sleep, but I'm not sure.

I think I wake up, but I'm not sure about that either.

I think I'm just… existing.

I could deal with having a father who disappoints. I think most men have that father these days. I think I could even deal with the fact that I'm just like him. That's pretty common too. The whole apple and the tree thing, right?

But what I cannot deal with is Ixion.

How can he even look at me now that he knows it really *was* all my fault?

Ixion appears in my bedroom one day.

I have no idea how long I've been here at Smith and Chella's house. Days, at least. Maybe even longer. Chella brings me meals. I sometimes eat them. Smith brings me alcohol. I don't drink it, but he does. He turns a chair to the window and sits there, sipping expensive Scotch, looking out at the view of Coors Field with his back to me, and talks.

Smith talks about his parents. About his childhood up in Aspen. His whole story is fucked up and sorta magical at the same time. He talks about the Club too. Why he agreed to sell it, though he says he had no idea who bought it and neither did Bric or Quin. He talks about his new career saving at-risk teens using boxing as the vehicle. He talks about his stupid dogs, and Chella's tea room, and the baby.

I think he just talks to like… put it all in perspective. Help me do the same.

But Smith has had years to decipher the meaning of his life. Over a decade since his parents died and left him all their money. And I'm just too new at this to fully appreciate it yet.

I don't miss the fact that he and Ixion are sort of the same guy with similar stories. I don't think my father killed Smith's parents, but at this point, who the fuck knows?

Anyway, Ixion throws the curtains aside, letting the sunshine hit me in the face. I turn away, like it stings. And it does. The light is so much harder to deal with than the night.

He says, "I have news for you. I mean, I'm totally OK with you checking out for a while. Hell, I did it for eight years so I'm no one to judge."

I huff at that. Because he's not a hypocrite. Never was.

"But you should know your dad died yesterday morning."

"What?" I say, turning over to look at him.

"Yeah, massive heart attack, I think. I don't have any details. Your mom called me looking for you. I didn't tell her where you were and I suppose she got tired of playing my game, because she finally just told me. So…" Ixion shrugs with his hands. "He's dead."

I sit up in bed. "He's dead?"

Ixion nods. "I'm sorry."

"And my mom?" I ask. "Do you know where she is?"

He shakes his head. "No. Home, maybe? You should try there first." And then he points to a suit hanging on the bathroom door. "Smith left you a suit. You should get up now, Jordan. Because…" He shrugs again. "It's over."

He leaves without further comment.

I spy my phone on the bedside table and reach for it. Find the battery dead. And decide to get up.

She isn't at home. No one is. I go inside to look around, thinking maybe she's just hiding in her bedroom being sad or something, but she isn't. No one's home.

And she's not at the hospital, even though I called up Lucinda and asked her to check for me. She left, from what Lucinda can deduce, right after my father died and didn't come back.

So the really sad thing that hits me now is… I don't know her well enough to think of another place she'd go. I have no idea where she'd go.

So I go to work. I park my car in the garage and walk over to the building, and take the elevator up and enter to complete and utter chaos.

Well, what did I expect? The founding partner just died.

I go into the private reception area where my office is located and find Eileen. She spies me, then says, "Oh, thank God you're back!"

The place is filled with people rushing back and forth moving boxes of legal papers on dollies. I spy the other two founding partners having a heated conversation in the hallway outside my father's office, and turn to Eileen. "What the fuck is happening?"

"Your mother's here. You should go talk to her. She's down there. In his office."

I nod, that awful sinking feeling back in the pit of my stomach. Because I just know something's happening. Has been happening for a very long time, I just never saw it coming.

I push past the other two partners, who don't even stop their argument to say hello to me, and stand in the doorway.

My mother is sitting in my father's oversized chair behind his desk, talking a mile a minute, handing out instructions to the five office assistants as they go through file cabinets and drawers.

"Mom?" I say. "What's going on?"

She stops everything and smiles at me. "Oh, good, you're back. Everyone," she says loudly as she claps her hands three times. "Get out. And close the door behind you."

I watch as all five people drop what they're doing and leave.

"Come here, Jordan. Have a seat."

"What the hell is going on?" I repeat.

"Well," she says, swiping a piece of hair out of her eyes. She's still Barbara Bush classy, but with a healthy dose of disheveled added in. She takes a deep breath. "I don't have time to explain the details, but the short answer is I've sold your father's portion of the firm to the other partners. And… and you quit, Jordan. I handed in your resignation and—"

"What?"

"—and you're done here."

"You… fired me?"

"No," she says. "You're not fired. You quit."

"But—"

"You don't want to work here, Jordan. Trust me. Just… just take the boxes I packed in your office and…" She shrugs. "Well, I was going to say go home, but it's being sold and we're having an open house this afternoon. Do you have another home? I mean, I'm assuming you do, since you don't live with us. But…" She shrugs again. "I have no idea where you live, Jordan. And that's not your fault—it's not even my fault, not really. It's his fault. And it ends today. So… wherever you've been staying, go back there."

I just stare at her. "Who are you?"

Which makes her laugh.

And that unsettles me more. Because… "I mean, Dad just died and—"

"Yes, that reminds me. Can you handle the funeral? I've already contacted the mortuary." She reaches for her purse and goes fishing through it. "Where is that card? Oh, here." She thrusts a business card at me and I take it automatically. "Can you call them and make sure everything is taken care of? We're having the funeral tomorrow. Just… you know, pick whatever you want."

"Mom," I say. "What the fuck is going on?"

"Later, Jordan." She frowns. "I can't today, OK? But I'll explain everything soon. I promise." And then she presses a button on my father's desk phone and says, "Can you send everyone back in, please?"

The door opens and all the people who were ordered out return and get back to work as I stand there, just feeling… stunned.

I turn and leave, still clutching the business card for the mortuary, push my way past the still-arguing partners, and go into my office. Eileen is standing in the middle of the room behind a dollie stacked with boxes. "These are all your personal things. And don't worry about me. Your mother is hiring me over at her company."

I blink three times. "My mother has a company?"

"A real-estate business, apparently. I never knew."

"Me either."

"Well." She shrugs. "It was a good offer. So I'm not unhappy about it. Do you want some help to your car?"

"Don't you think this is weird?"

"Super weird." She laughs. "But… you guys have always been weird. So not that unusual. Oh, and before I forget. Finn and Darrel came by yesterday and I sent them home. Your mother was already in control. So you should probably call them and let them know the game is over."

I just stare at her. Blink. Say nothing.

"Jordan?"

"Yes?"

"Do you need some help to your car?"

I shake my head. "No. Thanks. I got it."

"OK," she says, walking around the dollie. "I'm gonna miss you. Maybe you'll come by your mom's office some time and visit?"

"Sure," I say, even though I have no idea where that office is.

And then she's gone. And I'm left alone in my office with a dollie stacked with boxes.

I pack up my car, head over to the mortuary, and spend the next five hours dealing with the details of death. And then I go back to Chella's house.

Because I feel like there's no place in this world I belong but there.

CHAPTER SEVENTEEN

I attend the funeral out of obligation and feel like a hypocrite doing so. It's raining at the gravesite. Coming down in sheets, and we—my mother and me, the only family there—are sitting under a small hastily erected black canopy as the ceremony drags on.

Everyone else is huddled under large black umbrellas and it kinda pisses me off. That he gets a horrendous thunderstorm as the backdrop to his farewell. Something so dramatic should be reserved for people you're truly sad to see die.

I'm not sad and I don't know for sure, but I don't think my mother is either.

We stay there, sitting in our chairs, until everyone else has left. My mother reaches for my hand and says, "Your friend came to see me the day after you left the house that night."

I turn in my chair, the rain pelting the roof of the canopy so hard, it makes her hard to hear. "Ixion?" I ask.

"No. Chella."

Chella. "Why?"

"She was worried about you. And she told me some things. Things I had already found out about because when you left that night, you forgot to take your folder of evidence with you."

"Oh, shit."

"I didn't know, Jordan. But I should've suspected. Because when you came back from LA and joined the firm, I decided to get my real-estate license. And I did that so one day, when my nightmare was over, I'd have something of my own to fall back on. Oh, we're filthy rich, but all that money was his, not mine. And before you say it's half mine too, I don't want it. I don't even need it. I'm quite capable of taking care of myself."

"You sent me that listing last year, didn't you? For the garden mansion."

She presses her lips together. "I knew who she was. I suspected what had happened to her. And I couldn't let him sweep it all away by letting the house be sold in foreclosure. There was too much anger inside me last year. So I sent it to you and hoped. And you, for whatever reason, heard my prayer to keep their story alive, and bought it."

"I don't even know why, though. Why did I buy it?"

"Because somewhere inside you, you knew too."

"I didn't. I blocked it all out."

"I didn't know who she was, I just knew of her. I knew she got pregnant, that her oldest was your half-brother, and that she married another man and moved on. I forgave her because she was very young and very young people do very young things."

"She was the one who came to me in the cabin," I say.

"I know. I figured that out from your file. And I'm so, so, so sorry I wasn't there for you when that happened. I truly had no idea. If I had…" She shakes her head. "I'd have done this sooner."

"Moved out?" I ask, kinda confused.

"No," she says. "Got rid of him."

"What?"

"Your friend Chella came and told me what you did for her. She said... she said she owed you but she wasn't sure how to repay the debt."

"She told you I—"

"She said you helped her with a problem," my mom says, not letting me finish my sentence. "And she wanted to help you back. So I took care of it. Because I owed you too."

"You killed him?"

"That night you left... well, let's just say I was done being told to go back to the kitchen. And before you start feeling guilty about this, Jordan, let me just say one more thing about it and then I'll never speak of it again. He got what he deserved and it was a long time coming."

We just sit after that. Listening to the rain. Staring at the gravesite. Trying to understand the new world we both now live in.

And then she says, "Walk me to my car. I have one more thing to tell you."

"We came in a limo," I say, once I look around and see all the limos are gone.

"I had my car brought so I could leave on my own terms. It's right there."

She points to a silver S-class Mercedes and we walk towards it, no umbrella, but in no particular hurry, either. I open the driver's side door for her, then close it and walk around to the passenger side and get in.

"Reach into the glove box," she says.

I do, and pull out a folder. "What's this?"

"The will is being read this afternoon, but that's all yours now. You don't need to go if you don't want to. I just wanted to explain two things. One. The building? The one you wanted so bad? It's yours now. I made sure that was in the new will I drew up."

"New will?"

She smiles at me and pats my cheek. "The partners helped me forge it. That's what they were fighting about yesterday when you came in. I told them we'd sell them back your father's stake in the firm for half price if they put their stamp of approval on the new will."

"What's it say?"

"It just all goes to you. That's all."

"What did it used to say?"

"It all went to the club."

"What club?"

"Oh," she says. "Oh. I didn't realize. I thought you knew?"

"What *club*, Mom?"

"The Barrister Club. His club. His *sex* club. He gave all his money to them. It was part of the… deal, I guess." She shrugs. "Some mutually assured destruction pact they had. He sold you out so many more times than you knew, Jordan. And I'm sorry. I should've left and taken you with me, but that was a losing battle if ever there was one. He'd never give you up. You were his legacy. So I stayed. I did it for as long as I could, but the other night, after you left, and I saw what he'd done, what my staying had done to you, I decided I'd had enough. And then your friend came and told me she owed you. And did I have a way to help her pay you back?"

"And you did," I say.

"I did. I injected succinylcholine into his ass while he slept." She smiles. And if she wasn't my mother, she might scare me. But the smiles fades and so does the fear. "It's the perfect poison. He did die of a massive heart attack.

He was sick. And if I had left him alone, he'd be dead in less than a year. But if I had left him alone that Club would've gotten your inheritance. Would have gotten you, because they'd have dangled that money in front of you and promised you the one thing you thought you needed above all else. And even though you and I both want to think you'd resist and say, 'No, thank you'… you wouldn't have, Jordan. Because your father groomed you to say yes. It was inevitable."

"Holy. Fucking. Shit," I say.

"Holy fuckin' shit," she repeats. "He was a goddamned genius. A very *sick* genius."

"That's why he didn't want me to buy the old Turning Point building?"

"That's why. You already had a club. He didn't want you to have an alternative. That's why he bought it back when it went on the market. I always knew he did. I saw this coming because I was the one who made him sell the old club. The one your friend's bought. I've heard they ran it well. I've heard it was a nice place. Your father's clubs? They were… not so nice. So Chella didn't talk me into anything, she was just… a perfectly-timed catalyst. Please don't blame her."

"And Augustine? And Alexander? What—"

"Blackmail," she says. "He saw Ixion come home and was afraid the two of you would become close again. Not that way, Jordan. He was afraid the two of you would figure out the part he played in Ixion's family's death. So he looked up Augustine and Alexander and blackmailed them. Oh, they don't know anything about Ixion. They had no part in that. But your father knew the moment Ixion returned you two would grow close again. He wasn't worried about you being bisexual. I'll give him that credit. He was worried about you finding out he had them killed."

"But why did he do it?"

"Because Ixion's father found out that Ix took the blame for you. That's why. Your father couldn't—*wouldn't*—let that happen. He was a sick, sick man. So he brought your other friends back and used them to get to you."

"Alexander's family," I say, putting the final piece into place.

"They are as dirty as they are old. He was the only one to make a clean break. And your father threatened to take it all away."

"So they…"

"So they came. And they tried to tell you so many times. Augustine is a lovely woman, Jordan. We've talked extensively since she came to Denver. I reached out to her that very first week I discovered she was here. She loves you still. I don't know what you feel for her, but she did this for you. And Alexander didn't just go along. He was invested not only for himself, but for what you were to them. They didn't want to lie to you. They were sick over this whole thing. But I told them to do it. And I told them to trust me. And I told them to be patient. And they did. So please don't blame them either."

"Jesus. Fucking. Christ," I say.

"Jesus fuckin' Christ," she repeats. "I am a goddamned game player."

I just look at her and laugh. I can't help it, I laugh. Because my fucking mother is the genius in this game. She is the game master. Not me. Not my father. Her.

"And if there's one thing your father taught me over these last thirty-odd years, Jordan… it's how to play dirty."

EPILOGUE

So… weird.

Turning Point was finally mine. It was all I could think about for the past six months. And hell, if I'm being totally honest with myself, for the past year and a half since it closed down.

And then that day came when my inheritance was truly mine. That building was truly mine.

So ironic… that when all that finally happened, when I'd finally gotten the only thing I thought I wanted… I didn't want it anymore.

I gave the house to Ixion and Evangeline as an engagement present. And then I threw in the building as a bonus. Signed the whole thing over to them.

Ixion was always a good guy. He just never knew it. When he told me that story of why he was in jail up in Wyoming—that day I bailed him out and brought him back home—well, that sealed his fate, I think.

He's just a guy who wants to help. Just a guy who wants to do the right thing.

And he did, I knew he would

Turning Point is now called Safe Place. They partnered with Smith and Chella and combined their gyms for troubled teens with the six-floor building that is now sort of a foster home, I guess.

And looking back, I don't even recognize myself back then. Don't have any clue why I was so consumed with the idea of that club. Don't know why I'd ever want to go back and have sex with strangers.

Because the two people I belong with were always there in my past, waiting for me to forgive myself and come home.

I found them in LA.

I went to the Cheeseman Park condo, but they were gone. The leasing agent told me that the condo was under my father's name, and so it actually belonged to me. He even gave me their address.

So I found them in LA.

I was surprised to find them in the old Westwood condo, the very same one we all lived in together all those years ago. They told me they sold it, but it was a lie. Just in case shit went askew in Denver and they needed to lie low.

I don't hold that against them though.

It was a long, messy week of arguments, and accusations, and begging for forgiveness. On all sides. Mine, as well as theirs.

But the really cool part is that we got past it. And the even cooler part is… now I know what he whispers in her ear when he's driving her crazy with lust. It drives me crazy too.

I mean, how could I hold all that shit back in Denver against them? They were up against a master. My father made the rules of the game and then he put them on the board and told them to play.

And I owed them my forgiveness, though that's not why I gave it.

I turn over in bed to find Augustine's naked breasts in my face.

"Good morning," she purrs, still half asleep.

"Good morning," Alexander says, reaching around her waist to pull her close.

Our eyes meet over the top of Augustine's bare shoulder and we share a crooked smile.

"Good morning," I say, taking my turn.

Because we're a chain reaction.

A triple bond.

One of those rare things in nature that are held together not by attractive forces alone, but by something much stronger.

By love. And commitment. And friendship.

Maybe it doesn't work, but if we fail, it won't be because we were afraid to try.

It'll be because we tried and failed.

END OF BOOK SHIT

Welcome to the End of Book Shit! This is the part of the book where I get to say anything I want about the book and you can read it or not. :) They are never edited and always written last minute right before I upload the files to the distributors so there will be typos and you should ignore them!

So wow. 2018 started out with a twisted psychological thriller called Total Exposure and six months later the series is complete. Four full-length books in six months. I don't think I've ever done that before. Add in the Julie & Johnathan books (Original Sin series if you haven't heard of them) and that's eight books. I've released eight books in 2018 and it's only June. I have definitely never done that before.

So in a previous book in this series I said something in the EOBS like… We'll see if I can pull this off. (Referring to the story ARC of the Jordan's Game series) You never know if you can do a thing until it's done.

Well… I think I pulled it off. And I'm really happy with this last book. I think all the books in the Jordan's Game series came out well. Total Exposure isn't a book for everyone because it's psychological and kinda slow. But it's deep. And I think the poems in there are cool.

Pleasure of Panic was just your classic JA Huss romantic suspense. I mean, you could compare that book to Guns or Panic in the Rook & Ronin Series. Books I wrote back in 2014. And that's all I wanted out of it. I had just come off writing the second book in the Original Sin series with Johnathan and those books were intense. I just wanted Pleasure of Panic to be fast-paced and sexy with a big reveal at the end.

I had the most fun writing The Boyfriend Experience. I really loved bringing back the Rook & Ronin characters and meeting Vivi Vaughn. And the whole Shrike Bikes thing was a hit with the fans. And the book had a little bit of suspense but not a lot. Most of it was just two people thrown together though circumstances and hitting it off. The ending there was big, but not dangerous.

So Play Dirty probably wasn't what you were expecting. Some of it wasn't what I was expecting either because that's just part of my writing process. I like to make things up as I move through a series and box myself in a little bit. I've talked about this before in the EOBS of Meet Me In The Dark. How Merc (the main guy in that book) was in so many books before he finally got his own story. And how it mapped out his life in a very non-linear way. So when it finally came time to write his story I had a lot of constraints. And that's pretty stressful if you're a writer. You have to constantly go back and look to see what you wrote (off the cuff, most of the time) in previous books so you don't fuck everything up. You have to keep them on a timeline, because even though the character's backstory didn't start out linear, by the time he's the main hero, it IS linear. Everyone's life is linear. So you gotta go back and piece things together so it all fits and makes sense.

This is probably the hardest part of writing mysteries and suspense and that's why not everyone can do it. And I'm not saying I'm special, because you know, everyone has their talents and one isn't better than another. It's just… this whole putting the previous puzzle pieces together in an unexpected and new way is sorta something I'm pretty good at. My imagination sees around corners. I know how to fit that square peg into that round hole.

So I'm pretty happy with how this series turned out. My main goal was to write standalones and I think I did that well. Yes, there's some crossover because all the Jordan's Game books share the same world, but for the most part you can jump into the series at any point and be just fine.

I suppose some readers might think—Did Jordan really need all these books?

And I say – YES. Most definitely. I've been building his character arc since the very first chapter of Taking Turns where he was just a nobody. And throughout that series he grew, and got more involved, and kinda found his place in the world. So when I started Total Exposure he knew that place. He was kinda settled in. But he wasn't quite ready to take his own journey yet. It really did take all four books for us to see the whole story behind Jordan Wells. We needed to meet all the players and get all the details. So that's why I started introducing Jordan's father early. I always knew he'd play a part in Jordan's final ending but I didn't really know what that looked like. I just knew they had a fairly good relationship, Jordan cared about his opinion, and even though his father knew about his "games" he wasn't interested in flaunting his lifestyle in front of him. That's why Finn was on the lookout in The Boyfriend Experience. That's why I mentioned his dad's heart attack. I always knew his father was gonna die at the end of book four, I just wasn't sure how Jordan would feel about it.

And that house. I knew the family was dead in book one I just didn't write it into the story because I wasn't sure *why* they were dead. I just knew it was a pretty tragic story to walk into someone's house and see all their stuff left behind. And then to find out later that it wasn't left behind, it was… forgotten.

And the Club. I knew Alexander and Augustine "owned" it back in Pleasure of Panic. I just didn't yet know who was pulling all their strings.

Another cool thing that all came together was Washakie Ten, Wyoming. I chose that town back in Total Exposure because I liked the name, it was in the right part of Wyoming, and it was too small. Way too small for such big things to happen. Which isn't true. Big things happen everywhere eventually. So when Jordan decided to take off at first I was gonna have him go up into the Colorado Mountains. Aspen or Vail. Probably Vail because I write about that place a lot. But then I remembered Ixion was living in Washakie Ten. And I never did explain why he was up there. He didn't know why, so I didn't need to know why either. Back then, anyway. But people come to terms with things over time, and so Ixion did this (even though it was all in my head and not on the page) and he decided he was up there because he'd been there with Jordan at some point. Some good point in their friendship. So it all added up.

I was a little worried about Chella's baby being born in Boyfriend and not mentioning it. But there was no room in that story for Jordan's side business. It was all Oaklee and Lawton. So I made Jordan wait until Play Dirty to go see Chella. Don't hold that against him, it was all my fault.

And Chella… will she ever stop showing up in new

books? She has seven books now. Almost as many as Rook. I think these two must be my favorite girls, what do you think? ;)

There are two themes running through this book and this series and they are:

Be yourself.

And.

Don't quit.

Pretty simple themes that ended up embedded into some pretty complicated stories. And I think the last line of Play Dirty is probably the best last line I've written in a long time.

Maybe it doesn't work, but if we fail, it won't be because we were afraid to try.

It'll be because we tried and failed.

Because it's so true.

You cannot win the game if you don't play.

There will be a Happily Ever After book for the Turning Series and Jordan's Game. When… I mean, ideally it would be Christmas 2018. But we'll see. I have like seventeen projects going at the moment and I don't want to promise anything I can't deliver. And I don't want to stress myself out about it because I have been writing non-stop since October 2017 and um, yeah. I need to take a break from deadlines and pre-orders now. :)

My next book is releasing in mid-July and it's a Julie & Johnathan book. And I have to tell you – I LOVE THIS BOOK!!! Love it. Love, love, love it.

It's a true romantic comedy. Because holy shit, that fucking Johnathan is funny as hell. I guess there's a reason they put him on TV to make people laugh. We haven't released the title of the book yet but we're having a cover reveal on July 9th, so if you're reading this after July 9th, 2018, you're in luck. You can just go to www.HussMcClain.com and take a peek at it.

Also, if you've stumbled into this series and didn't read Taking Turns, Turning Back, and His Turn (collectively called The Turning Series) then you should really go do that. (Just visit my website at www.jahuss.com/the-turning-series to get the links) because you'll meet Chella for the very first time. And Smith. And Lucinda, and Bric and Quinn, even though they're not really mentioned much in Jordan's Books. And yes, Jordan makes appearances in all three Turning books. But most of all you'll enter the world from the beginning. See the Club the way it was and not the way it is now. Get a better understanding of why this place was so important to Jordan.

And one final thing before I go… Thank you, Jordan. For being the guy you are to the person we both know. And for lending me your name in these books and being a good sport about where it all went. The story you two share inspired me and that's pretty cool. And remember, it's all fiction…

…or is it? ;)

Julie

JA Huss
June 21, 2018

Thank you for reading, thank you for reviewing, and I'll see you in the next book!

ABOUT THE AUTHOR

ABOUT THE AUTHOR

JA Huss never wanted to be a writer and she still dreams of that elusive career as an astronaut. She originally went to school to become an equine veterinarian but soon figured out they keep horrible hours and decided to go to grad school instead. That Ph.D wasn't all it was cracked up to be (and she really sucked at the whole scientist thing), so she dropped out and got a M.S. in forensic toxicology just to get the whole thing over with as soon as possible.

After graduation she got a job with the state of Colorado as their one and only hog farm inspector and spent her days wandering the Eastern Plains shooting the shit with farmers.

After a few years of that, she got bored. And since she was a homeschool mom and actually does love science, she decided to write science textbooks and make online classes for other homeschool moms.

She wrote more than two hundred of those workbooks and was the number one publisher at the online homeschool store many times, but eventually she covered every science topic she could think of and ran out of shit to say.

So in 2012 she decided to write fiction instead. That year she released her first three books and started a career that would make her a *New York Times* bestseller and land her on the *USA Today* Bestseller's List twenty-one times in the next four years.

Her books have sold millions of copies all over the world, the audio version of her semi-autobiographical book, Eighteen, was nominated for an Audie award in 2016, her audiobook Mr. Perfect was nominated for a Voice Arts Award in 2017, and her audiobook taking Turns was nominated for an Audie Award in 2018. (She gets nominated a lot, she just doesn't win. She's OK with that. Keeps her on the outside where she belongs.)

She also writes book and screenplays with her friend, actor and writer, Johnathan McClain. Their first series, called Original Sin, released in 2018. They are currently working with MGM as producing partners to turn their adaption of her series, The Company, into a TV series.

She lives on a ranch in Central Colorado with her family, two donkeys, four dogs, three birds, and two cats.

If you'd like to learn more about JA Huss or get a look at her schedule of upcoming appearances, visit her website at www.JAHuss.com or www.HussMcClain.com to keep updated on her projects with Johnathan. You can also join her fan group, Shrike Bikes, on Facebook, www.facebook.com/groups/shrikebikes and follow her Twitter handle, @jahuss.

Made in the USA
Middletown, DE
13 September 2018